"I'M WORRIED ABOUT YOU, ROSEMARY!"

Trudy took a deep breath, then blurted out: "I've been reading. There's some weird disease. People lose weight deliberately . . . they can't help it . . . some kind of syndrome or something . . . it's in their heads . . ."

"I'm not crazy," Rosemary said coldly.

"I didn't say that. I only . . . it's dangerous . . . a sickness. Whatever it is, you're *doing* it."

"Whatever it is, maybe *you* should do it!" Rosemary shot back. "You could lose twenty pounds and nobody'd notice!"

Instantly, Rosemary longed to snatch back her words. She touched Trudy's hand. "I'm sorry, that was below the belt."

Trudy looked up, then forced a grin. "My fault," she said. "Friends?"

"Friends," answered Rosemary.

But they avoided each other's eyes . . .

Bestselling SIGNET VISTA Books

(0451)

☐ **FIRST STEP by Anne Snyder.** Her mother's drinking problem was ruining Cindy's life—or was she ruining things for herself...? A novel about taking that all-important first step. (081943—$1.50)

☐ **MY NAME IS DAVY—I'M AN ALCOHOLIC by Anne Snyder.** He didn't have a friend in the world—until he discovered booze and Maxi. And suddenly the two of them were in trouble they couldn't handle, the most desperate trouble of their lives.... (098544—$1.25)

☐ **I NEVER PROMISED YOU A ROSE GARDEN by Joanne Greenberg.** A triumphant film starring Bibi Anderson and Kathleen Quinlan based on the 5,000,000 copy bestseller. An extraordinary story about a sixteen-year-old girl who hid from life in the seductive world of madness. (097009—$2.25)

☐ **I WANT TO KEEP MY BABY! by Joanne Lee.** Based on the emotion-packed CBS Television Special starring Mariel Hemingway, about a teenage girl in grown-up trouble. The most emotion-wrenching experience you will ever live through... "It will move you, touch you, give you something to think about."—*Seattle Times* (098844—$1.75)

☐ **MARY JANE HARPER CRIED LAST NIGHT by Joanne Lee and T. S. Cook.** Here is a deeply moving novel and sensational CBS TV movie that brings the full horror of child abuse home. A rich, spoiled, and emotionally disturbed young mother, abandoned by her husband, takes her frustration out on her little girl... "Powerful, riveting, stinging, revealing!"—*Hollywood Reporter* (096924—$1.75)

Buy them at your local bookstore or use this convenient coupon for ordering.

THE NEW AMERICAN LIBRARY, INC.,
P.O. Box 999, Bergenfield, New Jersey 07621

Please send me the books I have checked above. I am enclosing $_____
(please add $1.00 to this order to cover postage and handling). Send check or money order—no cash or C.O.D.'s. Prices and numbers are subject to change without notice.

Name_____

Address_____

City _____ State _____ Zip Code _____
Allow 4-6 weeks for delivery.
This offer is subject to withdrawal without notice.

GOODBYE, PAPER DOLL

Anne Snyder

A SIGNET VISTA BOOK
NEW AMERICAN LIBRARY
TIMES MIRROR

This book is dedicated, with love, to my sister, Julie Norton, and my brother, Sam Reisner, and to Louis Pelletier.

PUBLISHER'S NOTE

This novel is a work of fiction. Names, characters, places, and incidents are either the product of the author's imagination or are used fictitiously, and any resemblance to actual persons, living or dead, events, or locales is entirely coincidental.

NAL BOOKS ARE AVAILABLE AT QUANTITY DISCOUNTS WHEN USED TO PROMOTE PRODUCTS OR SERVICES. FOR INFORMATION PLEASE WRITE TO PREMIUM MARKETING DIVISION, THE NEW AMERICAN LIBRARY, INC., 1633 BROADWAY, NEW YORK, NEW YORK 10019.

Copyright © 1980 by Anne Snyder

All rights reserved

 SIGNET VISTA TRADEMARK REG. U.S. PAT. OFF. AND FOREIGN COUNTRIES
REGISTERED TRADEMARK—MARCA REGISTRADA
HECHO EN CHICAGO, IL., U.S.A.

SIGNET, SIGNET CLASSICS, MENTOR, PLUME, MERIDIAN AND NAL BOOKS *are published by The New American Library, Inc., 1633 Broadway, New York, New York 10019*

FIRST PRINTING, AUGUST, 1980

5 6 7 8 9

PRINTED IN THE UNITED STATES OF AMERICA

Like a blind person reading a stranger's face, she let her thin fingers gently trace her own brow, slide over the bones beneath her eyebrows, follow the deep hollows in her cheeks, then touch the point of her chin. Her arm fell to her side, and she marveled at the long, long time it took for it to come to rest on the bed.

She was melting . . . floating . . . drifting. Transcended . . . above and independent of her body as if she were a vaporous cloud looking down upon it.

And yet she knew she was in control. Exhausted but triumphant, she had overcome everyone. She had overcome her body. She had overcome herself. But had she? She still wasn't sure.

Outside the door, the faint rise and fall of voices lullabied her into a light sleep.

Rosemary was starving herself to death. She was dying.

And she didn't know it.

One

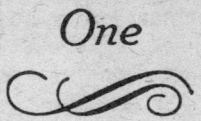

Rosemary Norton braked her candy-apple red "Z-28" Camero at the curb where Trudy was waiting. Her best friend had been away all summer, and now Rosemary realized how much she had missed her.

"Take me to the little red schoolhouse," Trudy said, settling herself in the passenger seat. "To the institution of higher learning, to the ivy-walled campus, to the infamous Ulysses S. Grant High School, otherwise known as San Quentin!"

Rosemary laughed. "Somebody would think you didn't like school." She wheeled the car into the morning traffic.

"Yechh!" Trudy said. "Let's ditch."

"The first day?"

"All days are the same for the doomed!" Trudy said, trying for a mock-stentorian voice.

"Maybe it'll be different this semester."

"Yeah, worse," Trudy said gloomily.

At the boulevard stop, they faced an enormous billboard. UGLY FAT MELTS AWAY! The sign showed a reedlike girl with a glass of diet drink to her lips. *I'll be that thin,* Rosemary told herself. *I'll be that thin if it kills me!*

Everyone considered her slender, but Rosemary knew better. She was not nearly as slim as the girl on the billboard. And no matter how hard she had exercised all summer, she hadn't lost a pound. It was frustrating. She was accustomed to accomplishing her goals. She'd failed at almost nothing in all her seventeen years.

Trudy sighed heavily and shook her head. "It's not fair. There just ain't no justice."

"What ain't?" asked Rosemary turning onto the boulevard.

"Here I am, wearing my Chemin De-Fer jeans, Gucci scarf, new hairdo, contact lenses, and sundry other secret and mysterious disguises . . . and I still look like me! And there you are—*au naturel*—and you're gorgeous!" She laughed wryly. "If I didn't love you, I'd kill you!"

"Thanks a lot," Rosemary replied jokingly. But she shifted uncomfortably in her seat, a niggling feeling of shame needling her. It was as if she were somehow using her own looks to detract from Trudy's.

She noticed a blemish on Trudy's chin carefully covered with makeup. No, Trudy wasn't pretty, Rosemary thought. She was too short and too plump. Still, she envied her for that uncanny ability to attract people. She was outgoing and witty. Rosemary sighed. She wished she had a distinctive personality.

"Personality kid, that's me. As in 'overcompensation,' " Trudy said with exaggerated sadness.

Rosemary started. Bizarre! Had Trudy been reading her mind? "But everyone likes you . . . for yourself," she said.

Trudy waved Rosemary's compliment aside. "I'm green," she said. "You're positively svelte! Skinny!"

Again, Rosemary was jabbed with a feeling of having betrayed her friend. She might at least have written Trudy more often. It had been a dreary, vacant summer. She had avoided the usual hangouts of the other kids when it became plain they didn't seem to like her. She was not exactly shunned, but no one ever called to specifically invite her anyplace. She had filled the long, tedious hours by herself, doing laps in the family pool, roller skating, reading, daydreaming.

"Know what I'd like?" Trudy said wistfully. "I'd like to have long, shining, black hair . . . green eyes . . . milky skin . . . perfect teeth . . . straight nose . . . willowy figure. In short, I'd like to be you."

"No, you wouldn't, you fool."

"I would, I would. I'd love to be you. Beautiful, successful, neat family You have everything. Your cup—as it were—runneth over!"

"So does your mouth," Rosemary shot back.

And the two laughed, warmly enfolded in their friendship.

After parking the car, the girls cut across the lawn toward the main entrance of the school. A frisbee whizzed over Rosemary's head and fell a few feet behind her. She picked it up and walked over to a group of boys lounging under a tree.

"Lookit that bod," smirked one of the boys as she gave him the frisbee.

Rosemary froze, pinned down by their open, leering, scrutiny.

"Hey, babe, let's go for it," one of the gang said.

"Check out the T&A," said another.

Rosemary self-consciously crossed her arms over her chest. The first boy made a wet, slurping sound and panted loudly while the rest of them laughed.

"Come on, Rosemary," Trudy said, touching Rosemary's arm protectively. Then she lashed out at the boys. "Get lost!"

Walking away, they heard one of the guys hoot, "Beauty and the beast!"

"Jerk!" Trudy fired over her shoulder.

Shaken, Rosemary could still feel the boys' eyes on her as they entered the school. Why had she worn these tight jeans? She should have put on her cowboy shirt instead of this clingy, jersey top. She looked at Trudy and admired her calm demeanor; nothing seemed to faze her. "Thanks for rescuing me," Rosemary said gratefully.

"No charge," said Trudy with a wave of her hand. Then she chuckled. "Gotta admit that was funny. Beauty and the beast!" She paused. "Strange, I never thought of you as a beast before."

But Rosemary felt like a beast . . . a freak. . .

They made their way through the milling crowd of uniformly blue-jeaned, T-shirted kids in the main corridor of the school. A strong smell of fresh paint and varnish thickened the air. Lockers metallically banged and clattered. Girls, who had seen each other only yesterday at the beach, squealed greetings as if they had just been reunited after a lifetime separation.

"Wow, what a terrific tan!"

"Where'd you get that top?"

"Hey, lookit that T-shirt: 'Don't read T-shirts, read books!'"

Raucous laughter, louder than called for.

"You look great, what'd you do to your hair?"

"Who's that guy?"

"Wait a minute, I saw him first!"

Boys traded friendly punches, exchanged affectionate insults, flung sexy innuendoes at the girls. Lovers, staring into each other's eyes, walked dreamily hand-in-hand. A terrified, frazzled-looking young teacher, clutching a sheaf of papers, hurried toward the main office. Maps in hand, anxious freshmen blundered into wrong rooms, ashamed to consult older students. Lettered athletes whistled and hooted at one another. And above the din, the school bell shrilled piercingly over and over in a patternless, insane obsession, as if to make up for its enforced silence during the long summer.

Trudy elbowed Rosemary as they approached a pretty, blond girl ringed by a knot of obvious admirers. The group fell silent as they came up.

"Hi, Stacy," Trudy said to the blond girl. "Hi, gang."

Stacy flashed a stunning smile. She was tall and model-thin. "Trudy!" she trilled. "Welcome back!" She looked over at Rosemary. "Oh, hi, Rosemary."

Rosemary nodded. She had the crawly feeling of being examined, X-rayed, dissected by the "in" crowd.

"Haven't seen you around. Watcha been doing all summer?" one of the girls asked.

"Nothing much," Rosemary answered. How could she admit how lonely she'd been with Trudy gone? "I kind of like being alone," she said.

"Yeah," kidded Stacy, "must be a real battle fighting the guys off to protect your precious solitude . . . or something."

The girls laughed. Rosemary laughed, too, but she smarted at Stacy's hostile remark. Why was she always the butt of their jokes? She would have liked to make a snappy comeback the way Trudy would, but she couldn't come up with one. All she could think of was that the other girls considered her a turn-off. And in some way it had to be her own fault.

They walked on, the crowd jostling them. Rosemary looked back over her shoulder. The girls whispered conspiratorially, flicked covert glances her way.

"They hate me," Rosemary said.

"Naturally," Trudy grunted.

Tears stung Rosemary's eyes. "Why? What for?"

"For being you." She glanced at Rosemary's eyes. "Look, Rosemary, you ought to be flattered. They're jealous. Snob-slobs."

Rosemary had to giggle despite herself and that encouraged Trudy to continue. "A nose is a nose, is a nose, and on him it just grows and it grows," Trudy joshed from behind her hand as they went by a tall and hawk-nosed boy.

They passed a sullen-looking bunch of girls dressed mostly in black. "The original bedroom bunnies," Trudy whispered.

"You're terrible!" Rosemary choked between bubbles of laughter.

"That one's for me!" Trudy was pointing to a great-looking guy down the corridor. "I'm not selfish. You can have the little skinny guy he's with."

Trudy pointed out and neatly captioned a few other kids as they passed: "Scuzz . . . Babe . . . Poindexter . . . knockout. . . ."

As they reached their lockers, a sudden flash of light exploded in their faces.

"Tim Griffin, boy reporter," said a handsome black guy, pad in hand. "Statement for the press, lady?"

Trudy rubbed her eyes. "What I could say to you ain't *print to fit!*"

Rosemary suddenly noticed a sandy-haired, good-looking boy who was carrying a camera and standing behind Tim. The boy edged closer.

"How's it feel to be back at good ole Grant?" Tim asked.

"I stand on the Fifth Amendment," Trudy quipped.

"Would you mind spelling your name, please, lady?"

"Come off it, you nerd, you've known my name since fourth grade!"

"A little respect for the fourth estate, madam."

"Bizarre!" Trudy groaned.

"Aw, come on, Trudy, I need some crap about the first day at school and all that shit. And you got the biggest mouth I know."

"Hah, and that's the Timmy *I* know," retorted Trudy. She looked at the other boy. "Who's your buddy?"

"New guy, camera freak, nobody important."

"Hi, I'm Trudy, the mouth," she said, introducing them. "This is Rosemary, the total babe."

"Jason. Jason Galanter," the new boy said, his eyes fixed on Rosemary.

"Jason Galanter. . . . Jason Galanter. . . ." Trudy puzzled. "You're not *the* Jason Galanter?"

"The same," he answered. "Once removed, of course. The first and only son of Jason Galanter, Senior."

"Wow!" Trudy was impressed. "Your dad's the famous foreign correspondent?"

Jason grinned proudly. "Photojournalist," he corrected.

The school bell vibrated an extra-long, insistent, peal. Trudy looked at her watch. "Hate to tear myself away from you big-time reporters, but I gotta get to class." She started off. "See you later, Rosemary."

"Hey, you never gave me any statement!" Tim yelled, running after her.

"Think he'll get his statement?" Jason asked after the others had gone.

"From Trudy? How can he avoid it?"

They both laughed. Then their eyes locked and they were silent.

Flustered, Rosemary looked down, turning her eyes to

his camera. "Nikon. Nice camera." She didn't know what else to say.

"You into photography?"

"No."

"Then what?"

"I don't know. Nothing, really. I skate a lot."

"Hey," said Jason. "Me, too. Doing a layout on skating for the next issue."

The tardy bell resounded fitfully. Rosemary slammed her locker shut. When she turned, she found herself face-to-face with Jason once more. Surprised, she backed up against the locker.

"Where do you do it?" Jason smiled.

Rosemary felt the blood rise to her face. Trapped against the locker, she could hear her heart pound. Was he going to make a grab for her?

"Skate . . . where do you skate?"

"Oh, skate . . . at Venice Beach, mostly."

What is the matter with me? she thought. *Why can't I even talk to a boy without falling apart?* "I . . . I'd better go," she stammered.

Jason moved aside to let her pass. Feeling stupid and confused, she started away. Was he watching her? Sizing her up? He was probably onto her already. Had her pegged for a sad case, a loser.

"Rosemary . . . Rosie!" he called.

Wheeling around, she heard a click and was caught in the flash of his camera. Tiny, shining lights danced before her eyes.

"Oh, please," she said. "You won't print that!"

"No way."

"Then why. . . ?"

Jason grinned. "To keep. For me. To remember when we met."

Rosemary hurried to her class. Why did he really want her picture? Was he handing her a line? Putting her on? Was he going to pass the photo around for all the boys to leer at?

Or did he truly want to remember when they met?

Two

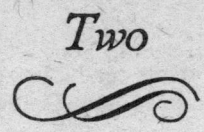

Still dripping from her shower, Rosemary stood in profile and gazed at her reflection. Her rear protruded obscenely; her breasts were huge, disgusting mounds. She turned full-face to the mirror. Stomach. Why hadn't she noticed that bulge before? Yes, that boy under the tree at school was right. T & A . . . T & A. She was fat . . . grotesque . . . revolting.

She thought of Stacy. Tight-muscled, thin . . . emaculate. Compared to her, Rosemary was an obese, corpulent slob.

She sucked in her stomach and vowed that starting that very moment, she was going to be different . . . a new person. She would make herself sleek, thin, clean! Like Stacy.

After drying, she weighed herself on the bathroom scale. Then she went to her desk and took out a brand-new green notebook. On the first page she wrote down the following: *Date, September 11; Hour, 7:00 a.m.; Height, 5'6"; Weight, 108 lbs.*

The family was already at breakfast when she finally came down.

Her father looked up from his newspaper and smiled. "Here she comes . . ." he sang out in his corny Bert Parks imitation, "Miss Ameeericaaa. . . ."

Rosemary forced herself to smile back and nodded to the others. She knew what was coming next and got ready to pretend it was funny.

"How's the most beautiful girl of all my boys?" her father said.

Rosemary smothered a wave of irritation. "Fine." She took her place at the table.

"Hey, how about old ugly me?" joshed her sister, Amy. "Am I an orphan or something?"

Uneasily, Rosemary poured herself a cup of coffee.

"You," answered Dad, "are one of my very favorite daughters. And one of the smartest, as well."

"Guess I run a distant third around here," her mother said, joining in. She shot a look at her husband, and then she and Amy exchanged knowing glances.

As her father buried his face back into the newspaper, Rosemary felt strangely severed, disconnected from the family. It was as if she were caught in a rip tide, a dangerous undercurrent, washing her away from a safe, familiar shore.

The closed expressions on both Mom's and Amy's faces were identical; clones of inscrutable, impenetrable secrecy.

Amy, nearly five years her senior, was as protective of Rosemary as her mother. Sometimes it was hard for Rosemary to tell where "mother" left off and "sister" began. Now, she began to feel a family mystery from which she was totally shut off. The two were like the mother-daughter look-alikes she had often seen on television commercials. Both had short, brown hair cut in easy-to-care-for styles. Their plain features were softly rounded, as were their full, earth-mother figures.

Mom handed her a plate. "Eggs, Angelface? Cereal?"

Should she take the food? That would ruin her diet before she even got started. But if she refused, Mom would be offended. She'd gone to all the trouble to fix it. "Eggs will be fine," she said smiling.

She looked about at her family, framing their faces in her glance. *They're all so giving . . . without reason. Without knowing why or what for.*

"Here you are, Angelface," Mom said, ladling eggs onto the plate.

Rosemary bristled. She wished Mom wouldn't call her that idiotic nickname. All three of them treated her like some kind of fragile ornament. They made her feel like a parasite. For a moment, she would have liked them all to disappear.

Then, flooded with instant guilt, horrified at her terrible thoughts, her face reddened and she stirred her coffee determinedly. She didn't deserve to have such a loving family.

Amy touched her arm. "The beginning of the semester's always a little rough," she said.

Rosemary reached for a piece of toast, shrugging off Amy's hand. Puzzled, Amy looked back at her closely.

"Beginning of the semester," her mother dreamily murmured. "Plaid skirts . . . saddle shoes . . . fall in the air . . . football . . ." She paused. "And the boys . . . ah, the boys. . . ."

Dad rose abruptly. "Got a meeting. Better get going." He kissed his wife lightly on the cheek, threw a kiss to his daughters.

"Have a good day," Mom said.

"Right. You, too."

Rosemary watched her father leave the room. She shuddered. Would he be so pleasant if he guessed what she'd been thinking?

They used to play a game like that. She and Dad. The thinking game. Staring into her coffee cup, it came back to her, the ritual they used to perform when she was very little. He'd lift her onto his lap, cup her chin in his hand, look deeply into her eyes, and very, very seriously say: "What do you think, Rosemary?"

"About what, Daddy?"

"What do you want to think about?"

"I want to think about stars."

"All right, what do you think about stars?"

And Rosemary would tease: "I think there's a candle behind each star."

"And I think you may be right."

"Tommy spit on me today. I think he's a baby," Rosemary would say.

"Yes, Rosemary, I think so, too."

"I think I can read as good as Amy."

"I think she's had more time to learn."

GOODBYE, PAPER DOLL

"I think I can read *almost* as good as Amy."

"What else do you think?"

"I think . . . I think. . . ." Rosemary would say, trying to stretch the game.

"What do you think, Rosemary?"

"I think you're a teddy bear . . . no, a lion!" She would giggle.

"I think you're a doll . . . no, a Christmas angel on top of the tree."

And now she'd laugh so hard she could hardly breath. "I think . . . I think . . . I think I love you, Daddy!"

And Daddy would stand and toss her high in the air, and before he'd put her down, he'd shout, "And I think I love you, too!"

How long since Dad had asked her what she thought about, Rosemary mused. The hugging, the talking . . . when did it stop . . . why? What had she done to spoil everything? What had she. . . . Oh, my God, she thought, what if he still *knew* what she was thinking? A sharp point of panic quivered at the pit of her stomach.

"Rosemary?" Mom was saying.

Rosemary blinked, looked at Mom vacantly.

"You've been daydreaming again." She turned to Amy. "It's her age," Mom said in a confidential tone.

Embarrassed, Rosemary toyed with her food.

Mom consulted a list. "Shall we do the rest of your shopping this morning, Amy? That'll take care of the clothes bit. Then if you like, I'll help you pack in the afternoon." Her voice quavered. "Oh, Amy, I'm going to miss you! Such a short visit. I hate it when you have to go back to college."

"Still? After almost four years?" Then in mock seriousness Amy said, "From my lofty position as a sociology major, I'd say, Mrs. Norton, that you're suffering from the 'empty-nest syndrome.'"

Rosemary's chair grated over the sound of Mom's laughter as she quickly stood up. "See you later," she said in a small, hurried voice.

She noticed Amy's sudden, pained expression.

Mom began stacking the breakfast dishes. "Be home on time, Angelface. It's your sister's farewell dinner."

Rosemary was hurrying down the walk when Amy caught up to her. "I'm sorry," said Amy. "I didn't mean ... I was only kidding."

"It's okay," smiled Rosemary.

"It's *not* okay! I hurt you. That dumb crack about the empty nest ... as if *you* still won't be here!" She groaned and clapped her hand to her forehead. "Boy, some social worker I'm going to make!"

"It's all right, don't worry about it."

"What's wrong?" Amy said.

"Nothing." Rosemary looked away.

"You didn't eat. You didn't touch your breakfast."

"Not hungry."

"Hey, you're talking to your big sister, remember?"

Rosemary looked at her. Her big sister. Her keeper was more like it.

"Well?" Amy said.

"I'm dieting, that's all."

Amy laughed. "You gotta be kidding!" She paused and scrutinized her sister. "You're *not* kidding, are you?"

Rosemary turned. "I'll be late," she said. She unlocked the car, knowing Amy was still standing there, watching her. She shouldn't have been so short with her sister. She had no reason to be so rough on her. She ran back and gave her a hug.

When they finally parted, Amy caught onto her hand. "Listen, tonight, after the folks go to bed, let's talk."

Rosemary flashed a loving smile. "No need—it's like you said—beginning of school and all that jazz. I'm fine. Really."

"Well, remember if you ever *do* want to talk, I'm just down in San Diego."

"Okay. Sure," Rosemary said.

Three

Outwardly, nothing changed as the days went by. Rosemary had fallen into the school routine as she had always done. She remained always on the periphery of the various cliques, with Trudy her only liaison with the "in" group. Despite Trudy's invitations to join into her activities, Rosemary usually declined. And yet she felt an unreasoning resentment at Trudy's involvements. But she told herself she had no time to waste on unimportant events, on shallow people. She preferred to remain an all-A student, concentrating on her work, and especially on her exercise program, and on Trudy only when she had a little spare time.

When the first issue of the school newspaper came out, Rosemary was relieved to find that the picture Jason had taken was not among its pages. Because he was a senior and she a junior, they had no classes together, but somehow they seemed to run into each other several times a day. Curious, she was tempted to ask him what he had done with the photo, but she never got up enough courage. She was afraid she might find out he'd made copies and handed them out to his friends as a perfect example of T & A. So whenever she saw him, she did her best to get away fast.

Weekdays, she tolerated school, but weekends were the best. On this particular Saturday she awoke to a blue-and-golden day. Perfect weather to skate at the beach.

She showered and stepped on the scale. Then, as was her now entrenched daily habit, she wrote in her small green notebook: *September 22; Hour, 7 a.m.; Weight, 105 lbs.* She frowned. She had lost only three pounds since she began her diet. She'd have to be even more careful about eating, and exercise more. Well, she'd skate extra long today, and not stop for any lunch at all.

The kitchen was deserted. Saturday was her parents' day to sleep late. She drank a small glass of orange juice, then wrote a note to leave on the table: "Went to the beach. See you before dark. R."

Thoughtfully, Rosemary surveyed the immaculate, eat-off-the-floor kitchen. Then she swished some milk into the bottom of a glass and put it into the sink along with the juice glass. She made some toast, crumbled a corner of it into a plate, and stuffed the rest into the garbage disposal. She broke an egg into the disposal, being careful to leave some evidence of the shell in the sink.

There. That would keep Mom off her back. Her mother had been on a "You-don't-eat-enough-to-keep-a-bird-alive" kick lately. But what Mom failed to realize was that she had never felt better in her life. She felt energetic, alive, disciplined. For the first time that she could remember, she was doing something by herself . . . for herself.

It was faster to take the freeway to Venice Beach, but she chose to drive slowly over the mountain pass. She loved to drive. She loved her car. It had been a gift from her parents on her sixteenth birthday.

The day showed all signs of being a typically hot one, but at this hour of the morning the air was still softly cool and smogless. She began to relax.

She could never take this drive without marveling at living in such beautiful extravagance . . . a city of such sharp contrasts. The narrow road took her past green, rolling foothills. A stream playfully shouldered the road over the mountain almost as far as the beach itself. As if it were playing hide-and-seek, the stream hid behind boulders, dove underground for some of the way only to reappear unexpectedly on the other side of the road, and passing demurely across the pebbles, it continued frolicking alongside until it disappeared completely into a deep gorge.

When she was nearly at the summit, Rosemary stopped

the car in a view turn-off. The entire San Fernando Valley sprawled out before her, the sun catching glints of turquoise in backyard swimming pools, like odd-shaped splinters of broken bottle glass. And in the background, the Santa Susana Range in the north revealed every wrinkle on its tanned face. Soon, its heights would be masked with snow, but now its back was shawled warmly by the Mojave Desert, its face cooled by gentle Pacific breezes.

Standing at the edge of the cliff, she felt in command . . . powerful. She remembered playing with the tiny pieces of the toy "town" she had received one Christmas when she was quite little. For hours on end she had arranged and rearranged the locations of the church, the general store, the barn, the animals, the miniature plastic people. She would put everything in its perfect place only to find something in the town out of sync the next day. Then she would happily begin all over again. The barn would go here, the church there, the people where they belonged.

She smiled. Somewhere in the garage loft there was an old clothes hamper still crammed with a jumble of lakes and ponds made of mirror, a one-room schoolhouse, a railroad station, a town hall.

One day—maybe next Christmas—she'd take down the hamper and set up her toy town again. She sighed and got back into the car.

At the top of the pass, Rosemary drove through a short tunnel, and was suddenly plunged into a kind of moonscape. As if to create a deliberate shock effect, the gentle, green terrain dropped its innocent facade to expose its stark, naked boulders, its jagged, granite outcroppings. Both sides of its road sheered cruelly down deep gorges. Even its roadside signs changed from polite cautions of "No Smoking," or "Fire Area," to sharp warnings of "Watch For Falling Rocks," "Slippery When Wet," "Dangerous Curves Ahead."

Then, rounding a hairpin curve, Rosemary was abruptly faced with a brilliant sheet of blue, the smooth sea and silken sky seamless where the one ended and the other began. She had come onto this scene endless times, yet she was caught by surprise as always. And again, she was astonished by her own startled reaction. Sometimes the sea and the sky were not so compatible as today. At times the ocean was covered with fog, the sky gray; other times the surf was menacing, violent. Still, Rosemary always had the feeling, when she reached the Coast Highway, that she had come to an inevitable conclusion . . . a kind of happy ending. At the bottom of the mountain the green arrow at the signal pointed in her direction as if to verify her thoughts.

With the ocean at her right, and the early traffic still light, the drive to Venice Beach was effortless. Rosemary thought over how she had changed since school started only a short time ago. The turning point was the day she had made to herself the most important pledge of her life, when she promised herself she would become the girl she really was, the person *under* her skin. She would be slender and strong. She would be smart and poised. She would get rid of every ounce of fat. She would be . . . it was hard to find the right word. Independent? No. Desirable? Not exactly. The thought of Jason flashed through her mind, but she instantly dismissed it. What *was* the word she was searching for? Superior? Superior! Yes, that was the word! She would be superior. Nevermore afraid. Nevermore dependent on her family . . . on anyone except herself. And beyond all else, she would be in complete control of her own body . . . in charge of herself.

By noon, the bicycle path was all but taken over by roller skaters. A hot Santa Ana wind from the desert had blown up, and Rosemary began to feel those familiar, awful hunger pangs. As she skated, she kept her eyes determinedly off the tempting snack stands and food vendors, but it was impossible to avoid their seductive, provoking scents.

Trying to make light of her intense hunger, she played a mind game. Eyes averted, she attempted to identify each of the specialty places she passed. Her nose told her when she skated by the hotdog stand, the cheesedog-on-a-stick shack, the fish 'n chips vendor, the pizza parlor.

Finally, her gnawing stomach won out over her will and she succumbed. I'll only get a little something to ease the hunger pangs, not a bite more, she told herself. She passed up a coffee shop and a bakery shop before she made her choice.

Standing before an outdoor fruit market, she pointed to an apple.

"*One* apple?" asked the aproned man.

"One," said Rosemary.

The man smiled. "Well, then, you must have the best and biggest one! Which shall it be? Ah ha!" he said, taking a large red apple from a basket and polishing it on his apron. "This must be the one. Beautiful . . . like you."

Rosemary cringed. She kept her eyes on the small apple she'd selected. "It's too big. I'll take that one."

The man looked disappointed, but he handed her the smaller apple.

Sitting on a cement bench, Rosemary slowly nibbled at her apple. She ate as slowly as she could, savoring every tiny bite. Down to the core, she broke the seeds with her teeth until all that was left was the stem.

Washing the fruit down with great gulps of water at a nearby drinking fountain, Rosemary wondered guiltily how many calories she had consumed. She must get herself a calorie counter. Then she decided to skate all the way to Playa del Rey and back to be sure she would work off her greedy indulgence.

By the time Rosemary skated back to Venice Beach, the Santa Ana winds were gusting the sand into miniature whirlwinds. Grit in her eyes and teeth, she did her best to avoid the bicycles and sanddrifts on the path.

Hot and exhausted, she narrowly missed a young boy on a skateboard, but in darting around him she ran into a rolling beer can on the walk.

Arms straight out, desperately manuevering to keep her balance, she was suddenly tripped by someone in her way and she tumbled headlong onto the walk. Skidding over the path, she felt her elbows scraping, her knees burning. She sat up, determined not to let herself cry out. The wind swirled sand around her head as she tried to get to her feet.

Then she felt herself being lifted and she was looking into Jason Galanter's face, his camera slung around his neck. "Rosie! I'm sorry . . . I was trying for a picture. Are you hurt?"

"You idiot!" Rosemary cried. She rubbed her stinging elbow. "You trying to kill me?" Her knees felt raw.

Jason raised her elbow to look at it. "Here, let me look. Oh, wow, you *are* hurt."

Rosemary pushed his hands off and started to roll away, but he grabbed her arm and steered her to the closest bench.

Tears streaked down her face. "Get away . . . leave me alone!" she cried.

Jason, hands on her shoulders, sat her down on the bench. "Sit," he ordered. "Don't move. My car's right here."

She would have liked to skate off, but it felt too good to be sitting down at last. He was back in a moment, carrying a first-aid kit.

Expertly, he cleaned her elbows with antiseptic and covered them with adhesive bandages. She clenched her teeth against the smarting.

Leaning against the back of the bench, her eyes tightly closed, she let Jason roll up her pant legs and treat her bruised knees. He spoke as he worked on her: "I didn't mean to startle you. I thought you'd seen me. I'm sorry . . . what a jerk I am!"

Then he was sitting at her side. "All patched up," he said. "Now, for your reward."

"You've leaving," said Rosemary sarcastically.

"No, I'm buying you a treat."

"Wrong," said Rosemary. "*I'm* leaving."

Jason pretended he hadn't heard her. He helped her up and led her in the direction of a tiny bake shop. "When I was a kid my dad always gave me a treat when I got hurt."

Rosemary looked at him. He was serious.

"My dad always knew exactly what I needed, whatever the problem . . . still does."

She softened. Just for a moment, he seemed like a little boy bragging about his daddy. He was almost reverent when he mentioned his father.

They sat on stools at the counter. It was good to be out of the hot wind and blowing sand, but the smell of fresh-baked pie made her dizzy.

A young, bearded man smiled down at them. "What'll it be, kids? We got twelve varieties of pie."

"Wait a minute," said Jason, scanning the menu scribbled on the mirror behind the counter. "I only see one kind mentioned."

"Right on," said the man. "One kind a month . . . that makes twelve kinds a year, don't it? This month is peach . . . homemade. Next month, pumpkin. In November, apple. December, mince——"

"Okay, I get the picture," said Jason, grinning. "We'll take the peach . . . à la mode . . . and coffee for me. What'll you drink, Rosie?"

"Coffee . . . black. No pie."

"Ice cream only for the lady?"

"No. No ice cream. Just coffee," Rosemary said.

Jason protested. "Come on, Rosie, what sort of a treat do you call that?"

"Had a late lunch," she said. "Thanks anyway."

Heartily, Jason dug into his pie and ice cream. "Wanna taste?" he asked. "It's great."

Rosemary shook her head. She wouldn't weaken . . . she wouldn't. She'd think of something else . . . concentrate. Let's see, she thought, if peach pie is for September and pumpkin for October, and apple for November, and mince for December, what would the specialties be for the other months? January—that might be chocolate. February would be cherry, of course. March would be. . . .

"If you could see yourself right now," Jason interrupted, laughing.

"Why? What's so funny?"

"You look terrible."

"Terrible? As in ugly?"

He nodded. "Look at yourself in the mirror."

She looked up into the mirror and saw that half her face was covered with a dirty, pinkish smudge. She must have fallen on the remnants of a discarded cone of cotton candy. Automatically, her hand went up to her face and came away coated with the sticky stuff.

"See what I mean?" grinned Jason. He wet his paper napkin in a glass of water and began wiping her face.

"I can do it," Rosemary said, taking the napkin away from him. "Who wants to be seen with an ugly?" she joked between dabs. "Why don't you leave?"

"I'm a photographer, remember? Behind that dirty face, that tangled hair, I can see something else." Now Jason's voice took on the same tone as when he talked about his father. He looked into Rosemary's eyes. "What I see is shining from inside . . . the real Rosie . . . sensitive, understanding, sincere . . . the Rosie nobody else can see."

She stared at him but said nothing. And this time it wasn't for lack of a snappy comeback, or the usual confusion when she talked to a boy. An alien feeling welled up within her that words could never describe. It was at once wonderful and terrifying, beautiful but scary.

Jason touched her hand. "Now, don't get startled . . . or mad," he said quietly. "Sit still . . . exactly as you are."

Then, with his eyes still fixed on hers, he carefully raised his camera and shot her image in the mirror.

Four

The glossy photo of Rosemary with smudged face and tousled hair was pinned to her mirror. She compared her face in the mirror with the picture. He likes *me,* she thought, not what I look like. And he'll like me even better when the real me begins to show through this terrible fat.

She rubbed some lotion onto her nearly healed elbows. It had been a wonderful week. She smiled, beginning to think in images as Jason did. A montage of the past events flashed through her mind, much like the pictures Jason had been taking. She could almost hear the snap of the shutter: Click—Rosemary at the Plaza Rink, skirt flared out around her, hair swept across her face in a candid shot. Click—A silhouette of her profile against the movie screen of the neighborhood drive-in. Click—Wearing a wide-brimmed Mexican hat, surrounded by the mariachi band at Olvera Street. Click—Caught in a ludicrous, froglike leap into her swimming pool. Click—Both of them making grotesque faces at each other in a self-timed exposure.

There was a knock on the door and her mother entered. She was holding one of her inevitable lists. "Going marketing," Mom said. "What can I tempt you with?"

"Grapefruit juice . . . unsweetened."

"I meant *food.*"

"Nothing special. Thanks, Mom."

"Dad won't be home for dinner." Her smile seemed forced. "But maybe he'll want something later. How about your favorite? Barbequed ribs, French fries——"

"Oh, didn't I tell you? I'm eating out."

"Jason again?"

Rosemary nodded.

"Not one of those fast-food places?"

"Oh, no. Somewhere very special. You'll never guess."

Mom looked at her questioningly.

"At Jason's house. To meet his grandmother."

Mom grinned. "My, my, sounds serious. Can this be love?"

Rosemary flushed. "Nothing like that. We're friends, that's all."

Her mother sighed. "Well, for heaven's sake don't insult the lady by refusing to eat."

The last gasp of the setting sun cast watercolors through the eucalyptus trees shading the street when Rosemary reached Jason's house.

A thick, flaking adobe wall enclosed the property, a handsome house with Spanish-tiled roof sat well back from the street, the doorway barely visible from the sidewalk. The old estate looked out of place among the modern tract homes adjacent to it.

From what Jason had told her, Rosemary hardly knew what to expect of his grandmother. He usually referred to her as "Countess." A long time ago, he had told Rosemary, his grandmother had actually been married to a Count . . . briefly . . . long before Jason's grandfather had come upon the scene. Rosemary pictured a fragile, white-haired lady dressed in black velvet, a cameo ribboned around her neck. How did one address a Countess? Or should she call her Mrs. Galanter? Should she shake hands?

The heavy gate swung open and Rosemary was besieged by three identical Irish setters leaping, sniffing, bouncing around her. Jason drew the gate shut, called off the dogs, and gave her a quick hug. As he led her up a curving avenue flanked by spreading Chinese elm trees, the dogs yapped playfully around their ankles. The authentic Mexican villa was galleried by a wide portico, scarlet bougainvillaea growing wildly up the columns and framing the overhang.

Rosemary stopped, breathless. "This is for real? Looks like a movie set!"

"Believe it. I get to mow two acres of lawn every week."

As they moved toward the entrance, the massive, carved door opened and the Countess stood before them. The first thing Rosemary noticed was the woman's large, brown eyes as the Countess openly stared at her. The Countess wore a colorful hand-woven skirt which looked as if it had been chosen for durability as well as design, and her rough-textured shirt sleeves were rolled up to the elbows. Streaked with white, her dark hair was gathered into a bun and held with combs on top of her head. On her bare feet she wore natural leather sandals.

"Countess, meet Rosemary," Jason said.

"So this is the famous Rosemary," said the Countess.

"Hi," Rosemary said shyly.

Then the woman smiled warmly. "Please come in, my dear."

Standing in the wide, slate-floored entry, the Countess turned to Jason. "I concede," she said.

"Hah!" Jason triumphed. "I told you so!"

Bewildered, Rosemary looked from one to the other.

"No special credit to you," his grandmother told Jason. "Good taste in women runs in the family . . . like your father before you." She paused dramatically, and with a twinkle in her eye said, ". . . and like his father before *him*." She turned to Rosemary. "That would be Jason's grandfather, you know."

Rosemary relaxed. There was something comfortably open and honest about the Countess. "Your house . . . it's beautiful," she said.

"Then you shall have a tour."

Jason tagging behind them, the Countess ushered Rosemary into the living room, its high, beamed ceiling giving the place a serene and cool look. The pegged floor was covered with an Oriental rug, its colors faded into mutations of gold and green. Modern sofas faced each other before the fireplace, but the rest of the room held furniture and artifacts representing a myriad of periods and far-flung countries.

One wall was devoted to prize-winning photographs taken by Jason's father, and to the Countess's delight, Rosemary recognized a few of them from newspapers and picture magazines.

As they passed the open French doors, Rosemary could see that all the ground-floor rooms faced an open courtyard, dotted with great clay pots of cacti and hanging flower baskets.

An ancient, gnarled live-oak tree sheltered a small guesthouse with an umbrella table and other redwood and wrought-iron garden furniture in front of it. Rosemary knew Jason used the guesthouse for his own quarters. In the background, the far wall was totally obscured with purple blossoms, their sweet fragrance wafting into the house.

Upstairs, the Countess showed Rosemary the small study with its corner, cavelike fireplace. Jason commented on certain objects—the pre-Columbian figures, the wall hangings from China, the icons from Russia—all mementos of his father's vast travels.

Featured on an old battered desk was a group photo of Franklin Delano Roosevelt, Winston Churchill, and Stalin, given to Jason's grandfather during the Second World War. Rosemary couldn't help noticing the boy's pride when she hesitated before the picture signed by Roosevelt.

The Countess led her into her own bedroom. Passing the huge hand-carved bed, she took Rosemary out to her balcony. Here, Rosemary could look down into the lovely courtyard, or up beyond at all the mountain ranges surrounding the valley.

On the way back through the bedroom, Rosemary noted some old family photographs in the corner, on the wall over a vanity table. Her eyes held on a yellowed portrait of a beautiful young woman. She looked in surprise from the portrait to the Countess.

The woman nodded. "Yes," she said. "It's me. Ziegfeld

Follies. A long time ago. Come, let's have some refreshments."

Wow, Rosemary thought, following them down the stairs. The Countess had been a Ziegfeld Girl! She'd read in books about the most glamorous of all stage beauties, and seen late movies about them, too.

In the living room again, the Countess sat down beside Rosemary and ordered Jason into the kitchen for her own special blend of herb tea. "And put the tea things on a tray . . . with the real company china," she told him.

Jason mumbled something about her putting on the dog, but his grandmother was adamant: "First impressions count, my darling. Let's try to be elegant . . . at least until Rosemary finds us out."

When Jason reluctantly left the room, the Countess said conspiratorially, "We'll never get properly acquainted with Jason in the room and continually trying to upstage me."

Rosemary shook her head. Had she missed something? Jason talked incessantly about his family . . . his father . . . his grandmother. He all but boasted about them.

The Countess went on laughingly. "Don't look so stricken. I adore Jason. And he likes me well enough. But I sense he'd rather remember I was once a Countess and conveniently forget that the Count found me in the chorus line." She sighed with mock gloom. "Guess I let the skeleton out of the closet."

"But he should be proud . . . a Ziegfeld Girl!"

The Countess shrugged. "You didn't need any talent. Just look good parading around the stage." Her eyes fixed on Rosemary's. "Oh, it was fun and exciting at first. But, finally, it became . . . demeaning . . . humiliating. I felt like a thing . . . an object." She paused, still holding Rosemary's eyes. "I know what the feminists are talking about when they say women are often dehumanized. I believe you know what I mean."

Rosemary was stunned. It was as if the Countess had verbalized all the conflicts she had been feeling about her own looks. The Countess was the only person she had ever met who understood how rotten it could be to be judged only by appearance.

Waiter-style, a white tea towel draped over his arm, Jason wheeled a teacart into the room. Rosemary was almost disappointed when Jason interrupted them. She had wanted to hear more.

"Are you pouring, Madame?" Jason said, teasing his grandmother.

The Countess poured the amber tea, which smelled of rose petals and ginger. Then she held a delicate plate of tantalizingly rich pastries out to Rosemary. "I'm sorry you had to decline our dinner invitation, but we did hold dessert for you."

"Thank you, no," said Rosemary quickly. "Mom fixed an enormous dinner tonight. I can't eat another thing." It wasn't exactly a lie, Rosemary thought. Mom *did* fix an enormous dinner, even if *she* hadn't eaten any of it.

When they finished their tea, the Countess excused herself to catch the highlights of the Dodgers/Mets game on television.

"She's a baseball freak," Jason said fondly after she left the room.

"She's terrific," said Rosemary, trying to make the shifts in her mind from fragile grandmother, to Ziegfeld Girl, to Countess, to baseball fan. "Your grandmother's one of a kind," she said in awe.

"Yep," agreed Jason. "She's the *original* original."

Rosemary got up and wandered about the room touching a metal sculpture, admiring a painting, flipping through a book of poetry.

"You ain't seen nothing yet," said Jason, catching Rosemary's hand. "I saved the best for last."

He took her through the kitchen to a narrow door leading down to the basement. There he ushered her into a fully-equipped photographer's darkroom and turned on the overhead light. Rosemary looked around and gasped. Pinned all around the room, on every available wall space, were pictures of herself.

Jason, enjoying her surprise, announced: "Ta da! A photohistory of Rosie . . . *my* Rosie! Like it?"

Tears welling in her eyes, Rosemary gazed around the room. Jason turned her around to face him. He tilted her chin. Then he bent to kiss her softly on the lips.

In bed that night, Rosemary fairly glowed, remembering how great her life had been since she met Jason. She really loved doing things for him.

She chuckled, remembering his delight when she had had a poster-sized blow-up of a picture of herself made for him. She had painted a thick, curling mustache and long beard on the oversized image, and sent it to him as a surprise by mail.

When she had made him a pan of fudge, he had taken it to school and urged all his friends to taste it while he bragged about her cooking expertise.

She had spent hours pouring over a box of pictures of Jason's father. The collection was Jason's most prized possession. While he had worked alone in the darkroom, Rosemary had delighted him by putting all the pictures in chronological order. She had been sincerely touched by Jason's gratitude.

Encouraged by his warm response, she often found herself trying to think up new ways to surprise him.

Rosemary was deeply in love.

Five

"I'll have to take the waistband off," mumbled Trudy, with straight pins sticking out of her mouth.

Rosemary grinned. "How much can you take in?"

"About an inch on either side . . . all the way down. Hey, stand still if you don't want to get stuck."

Trudy began to pin one side of Rosemary's jeans. When she finished tapering the jeans down to the ankle, she sat on the floor and looked up at Rosemary. "Why?" she asked.

"Why, what?"

Trudy stood up to pin the other side of the jeans. "All this business about losing weight?"

"Just keep your sewing machine oiled," Rosemary laughed. "You got yourself a steady job."

Trudy finished the pinning and straightened. She spit the leftover pins into a tin box. "Doing it for Jason?"

"He doesn't care what I look like," Rosemary said with pride.

"I'll bet."

"It's not that kind of relationship."

Trudy took a step backward, measuring the altered jeans with her eye. "You can take them off now."

Rosemary stepped carefully out of the pinned jeans and flung them onto Trudy's sewing machine. "He's a photographer. You know that."

"So? That makes him immune?" Trudy flopped onto her bed.

"He's not after my body," said Rosemary, her voice rising.

"Hah," scoffed Trudy.

GOODBYE, PAPER DOLL

Rosemary began to feel pressured, as if she were being interrogated. "I've sort of become his favorite model. Everybody knows the camera adds ten pounds."

Trudy stared at Rosemary, who was still in her panties. "If you *gained* ten pounds, you'd still be too skinny," she observed.

Rosemary pulled on her clothes and sat on the bed. "You're an angel. Thanks for all the sewing," she said, trying to change the subject.

"For nothing," said Trudy. "Look, Rosemary, Jason's a guy, not some kind of god. His sex drive is no different from the rest of the guys'. Sooner or later, he'll get you into bed."

Rosemary stood up. Rigid with anger, she walked across the room and plunked herself down in the chair by the window. "I can handle my own sex life."

Trudy eased her legs to the floor. "Okay, okay . . . sorry," she said, coming over to sit on the footstool. "You mad?"

"No." But truthfully, she *was* mad. And scared. What if Trudy were right? Suppose Jason did try to get her into bed? She knew Jason wanted her. And she had to admit, her own body yearned for him. But she couldn't . . . not with Jason . . . not with anyone. She couldn't explain it . . . even to herself. But every time she thought about having sex, she was drowned in a tide of terror that left her weak.

"I've got to go," she said, looking up at Trudy.

"No, listen, there's something else I'm worried about." Trudy took a deep breath, then blurted it out: "I've been reading. There's some weird disease. People lose weight deliberately . . . they can't help it . . . some kind of syndrome or something . . . it's in their heads——"

Rosemary interrupted. "I'm not crazy," she said coldly.

"I didn't say that. I only . . . it's dangerous . . . a sickness. Even their sex drive is affected. Whatever it is, you're *doing* it."

"Whatever it is, maybe *you* should do it!" Rosemary shot back. "You could lose twenty pounds and nobody'd notice!"

Trudy seemed to shrink within herself, a pained look on her face. Instantly, Rosemary longed to snatch back her words. She winced, feeling her friend's deep hurt.

She touched Trudy's hand. "I'm sorry, that was below the belt."

Trudy looked up, then forced a grin. "My fault," she said. "Every time I open my mouth, it's only to change feet."

They both laughed. Trudy stuck out her hand. "Friends?"

"Friends," answered Rosemary.

But they avoided each other's eyes.

Lately, it had become more and more difficult to sleep. Most of the time Rosemary used her wakefulness to good purpose. She'd spend half the night studying, doing extra homework. And when she became antsy after all the bookwork, she had hit upon the idea of doing calisthenics—quietly—in her room.

But tonight was different. She lay in her bed reviewing in her mind the ugly scene she'd had with Trudy that afternoon. The part about the sickness or syndrome or whatever, she easily dismissed. Trudy was only jealous of her willpower. She was forever bewailing her own weakness when it came to overeating.

And since she had started dieting, Rosemary had never felt so healthy in her life . . . exhilarated . . . in control. She felt pure and clean . . . energetic . . . superhuman No, she wasn't worried about her health.

It was the other part of the argument that wormed at Rosemary. The part about sex. The part about Jason being no different than the next guy, about his getting her into bed sooner or later. But Jason *was* different. Rosemary was convinced of that. Still. . . .

Her mind, like a movie projector, reeled off past scenes with other guys.

Replay: Her first date. Boy named Chuck. She's fifteen, he, the same. School dance. Mom more excited than

GOODBYE, PAPER DOLL 33

she. Other kids wear jeans. Rosemary, a skirt. Mom insists. School gym. Chuck holds her at arm's length. Has she got B.O.? Dance over. Outside her door. Chuck's suddenly all over her. Sloppy, wet kisses. Fumbling, hot hands. She's cornered. Sweat runs down his face. He snorts, writhes, jabs at her like a frenzied automaton. She stops his attempt. She creeps up the stairs. Nobody wakes up. She feels dirty, ashamed. A hot bath. She scrubs until her skin is sore. Sex. A total turn-off.

Replay: Another boy. Hank? Handsome. Girls jealous. Drive-in movie. No conversation. No touching. Rosemary relieved. Bored. Rotten movie. Next school day. Rumors. Whispers. She's easy.

Replay: Wayne. Older. Country club. Wayne shows her off. Parades her around. He laughs it up with other guys. They pay him off. He won the bet. Brought the prettiest girl. Never calls her again.

Replay: Rosemary's in love. Brett is perfect. He ignores her. She flirts. Nothing. Months later. Brett moves to Hawaii. A letter. He loved her, too. But she's so beautiful. He'd been afraid of a turn-down.

Replay: Rosemary withdrawn. Girls can't compete, avoid her. She keeps her distance . . . from girls . . . from boys.

Rosemary tossed in her bed, the top sheet strangling her legs. She lay still, her eyes staring into the darkness. Jason wasn't like those others. He understood her. He was her best friend. She could talk to him.

But could she? Could she tell him her innermost thoughts? Could she tell him about Chuck? Hank? What would he think?

"No," she said aloud. He thought he knew the "real Rosie," yet he surrounded himself with her pictures. He saw only what his camera saw. And the camera was not an X-ray machine.

Closing her eyes, she daydreamed: "What do you think, Rosemary?" she imagined Jason asking.

"I think . . . I think I love you," she could hear herself answer.

And he would say. . . .

Rosemary sat straight up. Dad! Maybe she could talk to her father. He had always understood her best . . . even knew what she was thinking when she was small. He would know how to help her now. She'd tell him everything . . . her feelings about Jason . . . about sex . . . about her looks, her diet . . . everything. Of course, why hadn't she thought of doing it before?

Dad was working late again tonight. Good. She'd catch him when he came home. They'd be alone. They would talk.

She extricated herself from the tangled bedclothes, threw on her robe, and slipped quietly down the stairs.

A dim light burning in the front hall threw the living room into semidarkness. Rosemary sat in the large wing chair in front of the fireplace. She wrapped the crocheted afghan around herself and tucked her feet beneath her.

It was already after midnight, but she wasn't concerned about Dad being so late. He often came home that late . . . or later. Since he'd gone into the commercial aspect of real estate, his business kept him increasingly busy. More often than not, his clients couldn't see him until their business day was finished, and afterward he'd have to go back to his office to clean up the deskwork. He spent his days conferring with architects and attorneys, supervising building sites, locating new properties. He was quite successful and very proud of his success. And rightly so. He had started in the business as an agent working for someone else only eleven years ago. And now he was "king of the mountain," as he laughingly referred to himself.

Rosemary smiled. Dad certainly worked hard. And he loved it. He played hard, too. And he deserved it. Whenever he could get away, he was off to Las Vegas, Hawaii, New York, wherever. Most of the time he went away on business, but he always managed to squeeze some "fun time" into the trip as well. As he put it, "My business is my pleasure, and my pleasure is my business."

At first, Mom used to go with him when he went out of

town, but she seldom did anymore. She had grown tired of wandering around by herself while Dad attended to business, and she hated eating alone in hotel dining rooms.

Mom never complained about Dad's absence from home. Rosemary suspected she rather liked the freedom of it: belonging to this club or that, taking classes, going to the health club, chairing committees. And when Dad was home, Mom seemed to enjoy cooking him gourmet meals, entertaining his clients, doing the *Better Homes and Gardens* bit.

Rosemary snuggled more deeply into the chair and laid her head on its arm.

Not fully awake, Rosemary heard her father's voice at the far end of the room. From his starts and pauses, it was as if he were talking to an unheard companion or into a dictaphone. His words were muffled, foggy, fragmented. ". . . no problem . . . yeah, great . . . like I said, at the airport . . . sure, baby, me too. . . ."

"Dad?" said Rosemary, struggling into a sitting position.

There was silence, then a few more hushed words and the bang of the telephone onto its cradle.

Rosemary stood up, rubbing her eyes.

"Who's there?" Dad strode over and switched on the table lamp. "What'n hell . . . what're you doing up this time of night?"

"Heard you talking," Rosemary said sleepily.

"You heard?"

"Could we talk, Dad?"

He stiffened. "About what?"

"You know . . . you always know."

"That's not your concern."

"But I'm worried . . . oh, Daddy, I don't know what to think."

"Forget it! Go to bed!"

"I've got to talk to you," she pleaded.

"In the morning . . . some other time."

"But I need to know. You're the only one who can tell me——"

"Nothing to tell . . . it's not important!"

"But it is," said Rosemary. "To me, it is. It's my whole life . . . my future."

"Your future has nothing to do with it." He started away, but she caught his sleeve.

"Please, Daddy, listen."

He sighed. "Okay. I'm listening."

"It's about relationships . . . guys taking girls to bed——"

Dad interrupted. "I don't want to hear anymore!"

But Rosemary couldn't stop herself. She had to go on. "I'm all mixed up . . . about . . . about sex! Don't some guys want something more than that? Is a girl's body all a guy wants? The way I feel it's so——"

His handsome face contorted, he took her by the shoulders. "Now, listen good!" he said. "All that's none of your business! Don't mention it again! Ever! You understand?"

Rosemary nodded, but she didn't understand. "You're hurting my shoulders."

He let go of her and stepped back. Suddenly he looked deflated, his gray hair and drawn face showing his age. "Go to sleep," he said tiredly, looking down at the floor.

"What's going on?"

Both Rosemary and her father wheeled to see Mom standing in the doorway.

"What are you telling her?" Mom asked accusingly.

Father and daughter looked at each other guiltily.

"Anyone care to tell me what this is all about?" Mom asked.

Rosemary flew past her mother and ran up the stairs. Once in her room, she flung herself onto the bed. Her hands clutched the blanket as she heard her mom's and dad's voices, from downstairs, rising and falling in anger.

What had happened? What had gone wrong? Then she knew. Of course. Dad was disgusted with her, with her dirty thoughts. He was embarrassed, ashamed of her. He didn't want to hear about his own daughter premeditating sex. That's what he'd said. He didn't want to hear her ever mention it again!

She crept under the blanket and made a kind of sheltering, snug nest for herself. Then she pulled the pillow over her head so she could block out her parent's voices.

Whatever it was they were quarreling about, Rosemary was sure it had something to do with her and her own filthy mind.

Six

Dad had already gone when Rosemary came into the kitchen.

"Morning," Rosemary said hesitantly. She noticed her mother's eyes' red-rimmed over her steaming coffee cup.

"So, it's finally out in the open," Mom said resignedly.

Rosemary's stomach lurched. She stopped in her tracks.

"Sorry you're hurt, but maybe it's better this way. Sit down," Mom said.

Rosemary sat opposite her mother, but she couldn't look directly at her. "Dad . . . he's disgusted with me. You probably hate me, too."

"What?"

"It's all my fault. Last night. I guess I went crazy or something. I pounced on him . . . told him stuff . . . a bunch of garbage."

Her mother didn't answer. Rosemary looked at her. Perplexed, the woman shook her head. "Want to start at the beginning?"

"Dad didn't tell you?"

"Let's hear your side of it."

"I was uptight . . . I wanted to talk to him. I waited in the living room. Must have gone to sleep. It was dark. Caught him off-guard." Rosemary stopped. Her heart was pounding, her voice trembling.

"Go on," said Mom.

"When I woke up, there he was. And I just spilled . . . let it all hang out. All my ugly feelings. I dumped on him, blabbed about . . . about sex . . . relationships. . . ." Rosemary's voice broke off.

GOODBYE, PAPER DOLL

Mom leaned toward her daughter, her eyes searching the girl's face. "What about the phone call?"

"What phone call?"

"The phone call . . . Dad's . . . the one you overheard."

"I didn't hear any phone call. Wait . . . oh, yes, that's probably what woke me up. Don't tell me I interrupted an important call!"

"Let me get this straight," said Mom. "You *didn't* hear what Dad was saying on the phone?"

"Just something about an airport. Why? What's wrong?"

Almost to herself, Mom said, "You heard nothing more?"

Rosemary shook her head.

"Oh, no!" Mom groaned. Then she leaned back in her chair and smiled.

"What?" asked Rosemary. "What about the call?"

"It's not important. You just startled your father. He was tired. Misunderstood you."

Mom poured another cup of coffee and slid it over to Rosemary. "Eggs, Angelface?" she asked brightly.

"No, nothing." Rosemary wondered at Mom's change of mood.

"Want to tell me about it?" Mom asked gently. "The thing that was troubling you?"

Buying time, Rosemary sipped at her coffee. What could she tell her? That she was contemplating having sex with Jason? Mom would only "there-there-my-child" her and give her the "birds and bees" routine. She'd heard that way back in junior high when she first got her period. Worse yet, she might react in anger and disgust as Dad had done.

"You and Dad fought . . . over me. I apologize," Rosemary hedged.

"Not to worry," Mom said. "Now, what's on your mind?"

"Ditto. Not to worry."

"Come on."

"Okay. Trudy and I. Had a kind of disagreement.

She said all guys are alike. We argued. Guess I overreacted. Wanted Dad's opinion. You were asleep."

"Have anything to do with Jason?"

"Really," Rosemary confessed.

"Want my opinion?"

"Sure."

"I like Jason. So does your father." Mom paused. "As for Trudy, not that she isn't a good friend, you understand, but a lot of plain girls bask in the light of pretty ones . . . in spite of their natural envy. Any girl'd count herself lucky to date a boy like Jason."

Rosemary reflected upon her conversation with her mother as she drove to school. Mom had kissed her good-bye and told her she was glad the air was cleared.

But something was off-center . . . still clouded. The air was *not* cleared. If Mom's quarrel with Dad was "not to worry," why were her eyes tear-reddened? If that telephone call Rosemary had interrupted was unimportant, why had Dad been so angry? Her mind going in circles, it was as if Rosemary were swimming in dark, murky waters.

The only thing that *was* clear was that she had created the whole mess, herself.

In the cafeteria, Rosemary slid her tray behind Trudy's. Famished, even the limp, pale spaghetti and lumpy chili looked good.

"Dog food," Trudy complained as she took a bowl of chili and two packages of crackers.

Rosemary put a small glass of grapefruit juice on her tray. Jealously, she watched Trudy fill her tray up with salad, a chocolate éclair, and a carton of milk.

Her stomach growling, Rosemary set a container of plain yogurt beside her juice.

Over the clang of the cash register, the clatter of dishes, the clamor of the kids' voices, Rosemary heard Stacy call out.

"Trudy . . . Trudy, over here!" Stacy beckoned, indicating an empty place at her table.

GOODBYE, PAPER DOLL

Rosemary followed Trudy through the teeming crowd of tray-carrying kids to where Stacy, with her usual entourage, held court. Trudy slipped into the empty spot, making room for Rosemary to squeeze in beside her.

Scooping up mouthfuls of food, Trudy still managed to catch up with the other girls on the latest school gossip.

Rosemary cast a furtive glance at Stacy, caught by surprise to see the girl staring boldly back at her.

"Been sick or something?" Stacy said. "You're like a stick!"

Rosemary shrugged and licked at a minuscule bit of yogurt on her spoon. It had taken forty-one spoonsful to finish her yogurt yesterday. Today, she would try to slow down to fifty before getting to the bottom of the cup. Hungrily, she savored every speck.

"Wish *I* could lose some weight," said one of Stacy's followers.

"Me, too," said another. "All I have to do is smell food and I've gained another five pounds."

"How do you do it?" asked one of the girls sitting across from her, open wonder in her voice.

Rosemary felt the girls' respect at her self-discipline. She saw their admiration, their awe.

"Easy," said Rosemary. "Mind over matter."

"Matter of *losing* your mind," grumbled Trudy into her chocolate éclair. The girls laughed. Rosemary flashed Trudy a look. She had sounded as if she really meant the crack.

"No, really. How *do* you do it?" Stacy asked seriously. Rosemary turned from Trudy and for the first time she could tell that Stacy finally saw her as an equal.

"Calories," Rosemary answered. "Take in less than you use up, that's all."

"Sounds so simple," Stacy sighed.

"It is," snapped Trudy. "Simple-*minded*."

"Shut-up, Trudy," Stacy said. "I want to hear."

"Me, too," said another girl.

"Yeah, so do I," the girl across from her chimed in.

"Some kind of secret diet?" Stacy pressed.

"No secret. Eat lightly. Exercise," answered Rosemary.

"That's all?" quizzed Stacy.

"That's *all* the *time*," interjected Trudy. She made a long face. "Rosemary's a sick person."

All the girls were looking at *her*, Rosemary, not at Trudy, not at Stacy. She was included, one of them, at last. No, she was rather *above* them, like a celebrity, a movie star or something. Here was a fringe benefit she hadn't counted on. Gravy. Better than gravy, she mused to herself. All you got from gravy was extra calories. Fat.

"I said it was simple. I didn't say it was easy," Rosemary said. "I count every single calorie."

"Well, I don't know whether or not I want to lose weight *that* much," said Stacy, drawing the attention of the girls back to herself. "Who wants to be a martyr?"

Sipping slowly at her juice, Rosemary watched them while the girls discussed their latest dates, their club activities, teachers, exams. And as they talked, forks carried mashed potatoes from plates to mouths like tractor shovels; cookies were swallowed almost whole; sandwiches were stuffed into wide, gaping gullets that yawned like Thanksgiving turkey cavities. Soft-drink paper cups flew to lips, and poured their contents into bellies already full.

Chewing, swallowing, chewing, swallowing, the girls—like mindless cows—were mechanically eating, eating, eating. Ceaselessly, inexorably in a marathon of greediness.

Pushing her unfinished glass of juice away, Rosemary knew her sacrifices were worth the effort. She would become known for her self-discipline, tenacity. Everyone would look up to her. She'd be untouchable.

She felt a warm glow deep within her and she vowed to be even more diligent from this day forward.

Trudy held the glass of juice up in front of Rosemary. "Finish it," she said.

Rosemary put the glass down. "Had enough."

Trudy's voice rose. "So have I! Enough of your craziness! You're going to kill yourself!" She pushed the glass toward Rosemary. "I worry about you, I really do."

All the girls stopped talking, their eyes riveted on Trudy and Rosemary.

"I can't," said Rosemary. "I'm full."

Trudy frowned. "Come off it. You ate nothing."

"Quit ragging me, will you?"

Trudy held up the glass for the others to see. "Nobody *normal* gets filled up on a few teaspoonsful of yogurt and a drop of juice. Attention-getting, that's what it is!" She put the glass to her mouth and drained it.

Rosemary felt her anger rise. "Knock it off, Trudy. I'm not a glutton like some people I know!"

Color rose to Trudy's face. "Then why don't you tell it like it is? Go ahead, tell *why* you're doing it! Why the diet kick suddenly!"

Rosemary stood up, afraid to speak. Afraid of what she might say.

"Go ahead, tell us common gluttons. It's Jason! You gotta be sexy for Jason!"

"That's a lie!" Rosemary countered.

"I may be a glutton, but I'm not a liar!" said Trudy. "Jason likes his meat close to the bone! You said so, yourself!"

Rosemary was stunned. She sucked in her breath. Then her fury exploded. "You porker!" she raged. "Big fat slob!"

As she ran off she heard Stacy's syrupy voice. "What a bitch! If I had a best friend like that, I'd hire me a bodyguard!"

Seven

Jason sounded excited on the phone. "We're doing something different tonight."

"What?" asked Rosemary.

"Surprise . . . you'll see. You'll have to be at my house. Come around to the back. Go right into the guesthouse."

"Why all the cloak-and-dagger stuff?"

"You mean you don't know what today is?" Jason asked kiddingly, as if he were shocked.

"Saturday, November third. What's so special?"

"I think I'll kill myself!" Jason groaned.

"Not before you tell me what the holiday is," laughed Rosemary.

"Thought I meant something to you! You're heartless! Cold!"

"Come on, Jason. What's the celebration?"

"Uh, uh," said Jason. "You'll find out later. My place. In the back. Guesthouse."

"Okay," said Rosemary. "I'll be there. But you sure sound like *spy versus spy!*"

"Six o'clock," said Jason. "Be on time!" Then in a hushed tone: "Knock three times." The phone went dead.

Chuckling, Rosemary cradled the telephone. She loved it when Jason got into one of his "little kid" moods. He seemed so vulnerable, so anxious for her approval. She knew only too well how it was to feel uncertain about other people's perception of you.

She thought about Trudy. Days had passed since their blow-up, yet she still couldn't absorb the fact that they were no longer friends. How could she have been so mistaken about anyone? True-blue Trudy! Mom had been right when she said plain girls were often jealous of prettier ones. That was it. Jealousy! What else could have prompted Trudy to turn on her like that? To humiliate her in front of all the other girls?

With Trudy gone, there was an empty place in Rosemary's life. But she filled it up by accelerating her exercise program. She no longer took her car to school, but jogged back and forth, increasing her speed and breaking her own record each day. She was satisfied that she was becoming firmer, thinning down.

And thin equaled strong. And strong equaled safe.

Rosemary glanced at her clock. There was plenty of time for a nice, long bath before dressing for the evening with Jason.

In the tub, Rosemary lay back and soaped herself bare-handed. She enjoyed feeling the bones of her shins, the sharp, thin edges of her concave pelvis.

She ran her slippery fingers over her breasts. They had shrunk somewhat, but not enough. Even lying down, her nipples protruded above the water line. She sank deeper into the water to cover the offending parts. But the water buoyed up her breasts, making them seem even rounder and fuller. Panicky, Rosemary sat up.

Mom had forced her to eat lunch today. She had really gotten on her case, threatened to take her to the doctor if she didn't gain weight. So Rosemary had eaten the soup and sandwich just to get her mother off her back. Thank goodness Mom was going out to dinner with a friend. Rosemary wouldn't have to worry about *that* meal. But she had probably gained a ton at lunch! She'd weighed herself only this morning, but all those extra calories at lunch could have been piling up fat more swiftly than she realized.

In fearful haste, Rosemary clambered out of the tub and stood dripping on the scale. Ninety-eight pounds! The same as this morning! Almost faint with relief, she wrapped herself in a towel and began to pat herself dry.

She would have to find a way to get around Mom's

prying eyes. Rosemary had already leaned too heavily on statements like: "I'm not hungry," "Had a big lunch at school," "Jeans are *supposed* to be baggier this season," "I'm walking to conserve gasoline." Mom was becoming more and more suspicious and more and more watchful.

But in a perverse, small way, Rosemary was secretly glad that Mom was being so observant. Whenever Amy was around, her mother and sister were like two girlfriends, excluding Rosemary from their closeness. And when Dad was around, Mom was so busy catering to his every whim that she seemed to forget Rosemary was alive. In a strange way, she rather enjoyed Mom's exclusive attention.

Rosemary felt better as she stood, wearing only panties and bra, in front of her mirror. She could easily fill the waistband of her panties with two fingers, and her bra cups wrinkled emptily around her breasts. She took off her bra and looked at herself from another angle. She was trimmer, slimming down. If not for the lumps on her chest, she could easily be mistaken for a child.

Another fringe benefit, she thought. She hadn't had a menstrual period for over a month. From the time she had been told about it, she had always hated the idea of a girl's being forced to bleed at monthly intervals, whether she liked it or not. She had dreaded the onset of the menses, and when they finally arrived, she resented the discomfort of sanitary napkins or the idea of having those foreign absorbent things in her body. She intensely disliked the entire mess. And she was particularly insulted by the fact that she had no choice in the matter.

Most girls would be alarmed at missing a period; they'd think they were pregnant. But Rosemary didn't have to worry about that. That would be an impossibility. Feeling smug, she smiled with satisfaction.

Promptly at six, Rosemary knocked three times on the door of the guesthouse at Jason's place. As the door swung inward, the scent of cooking flooded over her.

"Welcome to Galanter's famous cafe! Finest food,

GOODBYE, PAPER DOLL 47

cheapest prices!" said Jason, pulling her into the guesthouse. The two hugged.

Then Rosemary looked around. On her left was a round cowhide table set for two. It was resplendent with a lovely centerpiece of fresh flowers. The high, round-backed chairs, also made of stretched hide, looked as if they could have come from Spain. On her right was a tiny pullman kitchen, something delicious-smelling bubbling away on the stove. A brilliantly colored throw covered a sofa bed at the back wall. And across from the bed, Rosemary could see a door to the bathroom. The walls were hung with a potpourri of weavings, paintings, baskets. And photographs, of course. The floor was warmed by a geometrically patterned black-and-white Indian rug.

"Neat!" Rosemary complimented.

"Yeah," agreed Jason. "When I was small and ran away from home, I'd come here for a few days. It's been my home away from home ever since."

"Terrific. You were some lucky little kid."

"I know," Jason said. "The Countess has declared the place off-limits for herself or anyone else any time I'm in residence."

Rosemary's regard for the Countess jumped a few points. "What a perfect hideaway," she said. "And so convenient." She looked at the stove. "We're staying here?"

"Sit," said Jason expansively. "The surprise is yet to come."

"Oh, yes, the surprise," Rosemary said. "You never did tell me why the festivities."

Jason pulled out a chair for her and she sat. Then he went to the kitchen area, opened a cupboard, and brought a huge cake to the table. HAPPY 53RD ANNIVERSARY decorated the elaborate cake rimmed with tiny candles.

Rosemary was puzzled. "Whose anniversary?"

"Ours—yours and mine."

Rosemary laughed. "Fifty-three years?"

"Days, dummy . . . days," said Jason. "We've known each other exactly fifty-three days!"

"I can't believe it!" she giggled delightedly. "You've kept track of the days?"

Jason pretended to be crushed. "You mean, you haven't? You didn't even circle your calendar on the day we met?"

Rosemary's little green notebook flashed through her mind. "Not exactly," she said.

"Well, I'll forgive you, anyway. Help me light the candles."

When all the candles were glowing, Jason took Rosemary's hand. "Make a wish," he said. "And we'll blow them out together." He kissed her to conclude the ceremony.

"And now," said Jason. "We eat! I've been slaving over a hot stove all day for you!" He brought out a tossed salad and hot garlic bread.

"There's certainly no end to your talents," Rosemary complimented him, smiling. But she eyed the food with dismay. How could she not eat? He'd worked so hard to please her, to show her how much he cared for her. She'd *have* to eat! But she'd also have to do something to cancel out all the extra calories. Maybe she'd fast for a few days, not eat at all. Or, maybe she'd. . . .

"You don't like the salad?" asked Jason.

"It's great, perfect."

"Then why the long face?"

"Just thinking. Nobody's ever done anything like this for me before."

"That's because nobody's ever loved you like this before. Not the way I do. And nobody ever will, believe me," Jason said straightforwardly.

"I believe you," she said softly.

Jason smiled, cleared the salad plates, and brought on the ravioli. "My specialty," he beamed.

Suddenly, Rosemary was ravenous. The salad and hot bread had served to whet her appetite. And Jason's words had melted all her defenses. She ate with gusto, with a hunger she had never known before. She took more bread, a second helping of ravioli, and a third.

"Wow," said Jason appreciatively. "Either I'm a

greater cook than I knew, or you haven't eaten in weeks!"

Rosemary stiffened, looked at him suspiciously.

"What's wrong? I was only kidding! Eat hearty matey, eat hearty!"

Consciously slowing her pace, Rosemary gorged until she was at the bursting point. But at the same time, as if it would vanish if she lost sight of it for an instant, she kept her eyes glued on the cake.

Between gulps of coffee, she downed a huge slab of cake. Then, finally satiated, she sighed and leaned back in her chair.

"More coffee?" asked Jason.

"Stuffed. Can't move," Rosemary moaned.

"Good." He indicated the sofa bed. "Kick back, why don't you? Relax."

"I'll help with the dishes," she offered.

"No. This is my party."

Rosemary didn't insist. She was feeling marvelously lazy, like melted butter. She ambled over to the sofa.

"Now," said Jason. "Watch the clean-up crew move in."

"What clean-up crew?"

Jason grabbed an apron from the refrigerator handle. He tied it around his waist with a flourish, then waved a hand theatrically. "Violà! The clean-up crew!"

"You're flaky, know that?" Rosemary laughed.

He talked as he cleared the table. "One of the conditions of my lease on this place is that I keep it from becoming a garbage dump."

Rosemary kicked off her shoes and leaned back into the cushions. Admiringly, she watched Jason's movements, unhurried yet practiced. "How'd you learn your way around the kitchen?"

"It was either that or starve. The Countess is not your everyday *Cordon Bleu* type cook. Her repertoire runs from A to A. It stops at *apéritif*.

Folding her legs beneath her, Rosemary let her head fall back on the cushion. Her eyes were heavy-lidded. The warm room was still fragrant with the smell of good food and coffee. Closing her eyes, she listened to the homey sound of water spraying over clinking dishes. Her gloriously satisfied stomach, like a purring kitten, gurgled contentedly.

She felt Jason's kiss on her lips. "Sweet Rosie, my Rosie," he murmured.

And Rosie kissed him back, an electric feeling bringing her back to life.

Cradling her in his arms, Jason moved her into a lying position and held her close. His hands were on her neck, his fingers playing with the buttons on her blouse. Then he was kissing her shoulders, his hands stroking her.

Her body tingled as he drew her to him, and she pressed her hands down his back.

Again he kissed her, and she could feel him pressing against her. Between breaths he whispered endearments: "Angel . . . Rosie . . . you're beautiful. . . ."

She let his hands explore her, slowly slip down her sides. She mumbled a protest, though she trembled with pleasure, her eager body betraying her and responding to his touch.

". . . so smooth . . . so silky," Jason said, nuzzling into her shoulder. "I love you, Rosie. I love you so much."

"I love you, too," she panted, glowing with the warmth of his affection. She could feel the quivering of his muscles under his shirt. The scent of him was so nice; he smelled of masculine soap and talcum powder.

As his hand reached upward, Rosemary's head seemed to spin. She thought she must stop him, and yet she didn't want him to stop. Then he tenderly palmed her stomach and she grew almost breathless. His hand gently massaged, circled her abdomen.

"Rosie, my sweet," Jason said into her ear. "Little, round tummy . . . tiny little potbelly. . . ."

As if she had been plunged into ice water, Rosemary sucked in her breath. Instantly turned off, she lay rigid, her eyes wide open.

Jason stood up and began to unbuckle his belt. Reluctant to break the spell, he kept on talking. ". . . smooth little dumpling. . . ."

GOODBYE, PAPER DOLL 51

As he dropped his jeans, Rosemary jumped up off the sofa and ran wildly for the door.

"Rosie! What's wrong? What happened . . .?"

She pulled the door open and looked back over her shoulder. "I'm not fat . . . nobody's dumpling!" she shrieked.

"Hey, wait a minute!" Jason, at once trying to pull up his jeans and catch her, tripped over his pants, his arms and legs flailing before he flopped onto the floor.

But Rosemary hardly noticed him. All she could think of was her bloated stomach, her big potbelly. She ran blindly out of the guesthouse as if his damning words were chasing her down the driveway. ". . . dumpling . . . potbelly . . ." The words swirled around in her head.

As she pulled her car away from the curb, she could see Jason's image in her rear-view mirror. Arms waving, he was frantically galloping after the car.

Back at home, Rosemary raced madly up the stairs two at a time. Out of breath, gulping air, she stood in the doorway of her room. *Cool it*, she said to herself. *Mellow out . . . think*. She felt her stomach. It was distended, sickeningly stretched, like a balloon ready to pop. She was nauseous at the thought of how she had binged tonight, all the rich food she'd devoured. Then it came to her, a way to get rid of it. All of it. Fast.

But she'd have to do it quickly. Before Mom came home to hear her. Before the food turned to fat.

Rosemary hurried into her bathroom. Leaning over the toilet bowl, she stuck her finger down her throat as far as it would go. She retched dryly.

Then she heaved convulsively, and in wave after wave, she vomited.

Eight

Rosemary looked at the clock a half dozen times within fifteen minutes. Six fourteen a.m. She picked up the phone, started to dial, then changed her mind. It was still too early to call. She'd wait another half hour.

If Amy had to be away at school, Rosemary was glad it was only in San Diego, which was just a short distance.

It would be so wonderful if she could only see her sister again. She remembered back when Amy first left for school. The house had been so empty and lonely. At age thirteen, Rosemary had felt deserted, betrayed, even angry at Amy. Then, for a while, she had simply mourned her loss. She couldn't have explained it to herself—all the mixed feelings—but, at the time, it had reminded her of the first day Mom had left her in kindergarten. Rosemary had then been certain she had been abandoned, that she'd never see her mother again.

Finally, she had grudgingly accepted Amy's absence. If her sister had chosen to go away to school, she had decided she would have to live without her.

Rosemary looked at her watch. Oh, how good it would be to see Amy again, feel the comfort of her presence. Talk . . . laugh with her, the way it had been a long time ago.

Nervously, she reached for the phone. She had to get going. She'd make the call now.

The guy's voice on the other end was muffled with sleep. "Who? Slow down, don't talk so fast. Oh, just a minute."

"Hello," came Amy's voice finally.

"Amy, it's me, Rosemary. I want to——"

"Rosemary! What's wrong?"

"I'm coming down," Rosemary said, her voice quavering. "I need to see you."

"Oh, my God! Mom? Dad? Rosemary, tell me!"

"Everyone's fine. It's just that I've got to see you, Amy! I want to talk to you! I'll drive down! We'll be together! I have so much to tell you, and you're the only one——"

"Wait a minute. You mean, today?"

"Now!"

There was silence for a moment.

"Hello, Amy? You there?"

"I'm here."

"You wanted us to talk."

"What?"

"When you were home last time. You said we should talk. I can be down there in a few hours."

Again, a silence.

"Amy?"

"I'm listening."

"Is it okay? If I come?"

"Yeah, sure. I'll meet you on the bluff at La Jolla."

As her car sped southward toward San Diego, Rosemary tried to sort out her feelings. But her mind was as scrambled as images on a bad television set. *Thoughts:* Trudy. Fat. Jason. Food. *Feelings:* Fear. Panic. Anxiety. Everything was a jumble of food . . . panic . . . fat . . . fear . . . Jason.

But it would be okay when she saw Amy. About Jason. Amy would set her straight. Tell her what to do. She'd know how to handle things.

Rosemary sighed. She could leave it all to Amy. Right now, she'd concentrate on the drive. It was a lovely Sunday morning, and she had the freeway practically to herself.

Passing the oil derricks at Long Beach, the hollow emptiness of hunger pinched at her. She had gone through the "dirty dishes" charade before leaving a note for Mom, but this time she hadn't even taken a sip of juice.

She turned the heater on. So much of the time lately she was cold. Her hands and feet were perpetually freezing. She deliberately focused her mind on the oil pumps. Like mechanical teeter-totters, they fed endlessly, tirelessly on the dredged-up oil. Taking nourishment from the earth, they went on interminably, relentlessly. Without regard for space or time. They were infinitely unchanging.

Her stomach groaned. She really could afford to eat something. Last night's dinner didn't count. She had certainly gotten rid of that. But then she remembered the lunch Mom had forced upon her yesterday. Mentally, she calculated the calories: The ham sandwich, at least three-hundred-fifty. The soup, sixty-five. Good thing it was only tomato and not noodle. Not too disastrous. Maybe she'd stop at a coffee shop. But not yet. She could hold out for a while. She'd wait until she came to Laguna Beach.

But when she got to Laguna Beach, she began to play a game with herself. She would stop for something to eat at the *next* town. She'd wait until she came to San Juan Capistrano.

And at San Juan Capistrano she ignored the hunger pangs by trying to recall everything she could about the mission. Let's see, she thought, the mission was founded in 1776. By Father Junípero Serra.

Her stomach growled again noisily. The swallows, the swallows, she thought urgently. I must think about the swallows. What about the swallows? They left every year. They wouldn't be at the mission now. They come back in the spring. In March. Yes, that's it. The swallows always come back on a certain day sometime in March.

San Clemente was easier to bypass. She could still remember the summers her family vacationed there. Red-tiled roofs. Fishing off the pier. The Drum and Bugle Corps' Fourth of July parade. The railroad tracks running along the shore. Excitement when the beach suddenly emptied as every child within earshot huddled in the underpass while the train roared overhead. Arms wrapped around each other, Amy and Rosemary shivering in thrilling fear.

Now the ocean came into view. San Onofre. Nuclear plant. Grazing sheep, horses. Camp Pendleton. Marines. Flower farms.

And then Rosemary was approaching Oceanside. "Bob's Big-Boy Hamburgers," "Denny's—Open 24 Hours—Breakfast Served All Day," "Kentucky Fried Chicken," the roadside signs screamed to her craving stomach. She swung the car onto the off-ramp.

Rosemary chose a sleazy, unknown coffee shop. She sat at the counter of the nearly empty cafe. A booth would be dangerously comfortable. It would be too easy to order a full meal in the booth and then gorge in its shelter.

"Coffee?" asked the waitress.

Rosemary nodded.

"That all?"

"That's all," she said grimly. She knew she'd have to eat later on with Amy.

Hands trembling, she brought the coffee to her lips.

A fat, grubby man sat down on the stool beside her. "Feel like the works, today. Gimme the number five," he said to the waitress.

Rosemary took a swallow of the bitter coffee. Then, with shaking hands, she set the cup down hard. Some of her coffee slopped onto the counter.

The man looked at her and smiled. A front tooth was missing, his face unshaven.

Rosemary smiled weakly in return.

The waitress poured coffee for the man, then brought him a large glass of orange juice. She refilled Rosemary's cup.

The man drained his glass with a satisfied "Ahh" and a deep belch.

Then, a bit later, Rosemary's head reeled with the steamy scent of eggs, bacon, toast, and hashbrowns which the waitress served the man beside her. He slurped his coffee between great mouthfuls of crunchy toast, crisp bacon, and buttery eggs.

Dizzily, Rosemary stared at him. Transfixed, like a jealous child watching another consume an ice cream cone, she followed his every move.

Finally, the man stopped eating long enough to look at her. She flushed and turned away.

"You okay, kid?"

Rosemary licked her lips. "Fine," she answered coldly.

Gruffly he said, "Hungry?"

"No."

"Sure?"

Rosemary swiveled her stool around to face him. "What's it to you?" she lashed out.

"Stake you to a meal," he offered, bits of egg lodged in the gap in his mouth.

Rosemary stood up and began to dig for change in her purse. "I've got money!"

The man shrugged. "Sure. Nuthin' to me."

She plunked her money on the counter and started for the door, her knees quivering strangely.

"Must be strung out on something," she heard the waitress say as Rosemary reached the door. "Kids today . . . rather shoot up than eat."

Sitting on the grass at the bluff in La Jolla, Rosemary waited for Amy to arrive. The sun warming her back, she gazed down over the ocean. Tiny sailboats, like the tails of ducks with their heads submerged, floated across her vision. The bright sunlight sequined the sparkling blue sea. Closer to shore, kids clinging to huge rocks laughed when the waves sabotaged their grips and flung them into the water. Clad in shiny black wetsuits, surfers dipped and skimmed to the sand in triumph, only to turn and challenge the waves once again. Directly below her on the sand, two little girls were making a castle. Rosemary smiled when she noticed the bigger girl help the smaller one pat down her side of the mound.

It reminded her of herself and Amy during that first summer at San Clemente. The family hadn't had much money then. They had rented a tiny, one-bedroom apartment overlooking the beach, the girls sharing a sofa bed in the living room. All summer, Amy and Rosemary had slept together, spoon-style, cuddling against the fearful sound of crashing waves, against their unfamiliar surroundings. And in the daylight hours, the sisters had played happily side-by-side, never out of sight of one another.

The bluff shuddered as a mountainous wave cracked against it. The little girls' castle on the sand was washed out to sea. The two stood hand-in-hand, the younger one crying.

Fragments of an old tune drifted into Rosemary's mind. What was that song? What was particular about it? She couldn't quite recall. She watched the children below her scamper away as another monstrous wave made ready to fall.

The illusive tune persisted. And then she had it: "My Rose-Marie, I love you, I'm always thinking of you. . . ." It came back to her now in full force. Mom and Amy would band together that summer, and sing to her whenever she cried. And the songs . . . the songs all had the name *Rose* in the title! *Rose*, or *Rosemary*, or *Rosie!* "Sweet Rosie O'Grady," and "My Wild Irish Rose." All the songs—they must have been old, even then—had *her* name in them. And Amy and Mom would tease and sing until her eyes were dry and she'd be shrieking with laughter. Sometimes, they'd put her name into songs where it didn't even belong. "Rosie, Rosie, I've been thinking/ what a good world this would be/ if *Rosemary* was transported/ far beyond the Baltic Sea. . . ."

"Rosemary!" It was Amy's voice calling her, here, now.

Squinting into the sun, Rosemary saw Amy coming toward her, a picnic basket over her arm.

Before they reached each other, Amy set the basket down. And then they were hugging, laughing, exclaiming.

"Let me look at you! It seems like a million years since September!" Amy said, laughing, stepping back to get a good look at her sister. "What have you done to yourself?"

Rosemary felt a twinge of pride. "Didn't know it was that noticeable," she said.

"You're a skeleton!"

"Yeah," grinned Rosemary. "Here, let me carry the basket."

They found an empty picnic table and Rosemary set the basket down upon it. Pulling an afghan from the top of the basket, Amy spread it over the grass.

"Here, come," she said, as she lay down on her back.

And, lying beside her, Rosemary felt more content than she had in weeks. All was well. She and her sister were together again.

"Looks like a dish . . . a great, empty platter," Rosemary said, gazing up at a cloud.

"What? Where?" asked Amy. She followed Rosemary's eyes. "Oh, you mean that cloud."

"Not a cloud, nerd," Rosemary laughed. "It's a giant plate . . . empty."

"Uh, uh," Amy corrected. "See that other cloud . . . no, that scoop of ice cream settling on top of it?"

"Oh, yeah. That's one humungous scoop, all right. And look. There comes the whipped cream."

"Still pretty far away. You're reaching."

"Not that far. See? There it comes," Rosemary said. "Platter . . . ice cream . . . topping. . . ."

Amy laughed. "You always were good at making something out of nothing. And speaking of nothing, I've had nothing to eat since breakfast. I'm starved!"

Amy got up and went to the table. She began laying out their lunch.

Rosemary did her best not to pounce upon the cold baked chicken pieces while Amy laid out the rest of the lunch on the picnic table.

"Help yourself," Amy said, handing Rosemary a paper plate and a plastic fork. "Looks like you can use it."

"Oh, Amy, please don't."

"Don't what?"

"Please don't be . . . sound like Mom. I like how I feel. I like the way I look."

"You look sick," said Amy matter-of-factly.

"But I feel great . . . super . . . superhuman."

"You only need to be human, not superhuman," Amy said gravely.

"You *are* going to sound like Mom," Rosemary accused.

Amy sighed. "Let's eat. We'll talk later."

Rosemary scraped off fragments of fat from her chicken. Then she took a tiny bite. She chewed slowly, deliberately. If she chewed each mouthful twenty times, she could eat half the amount as that of the average person in the same length of time. She had come onto this trick right after her break with Trudy. While eating alone at school, she had filled the gap of loneliness by gauging her eating time against whoever happened to sit beside her.

. . . eight . . . nine . . . ten . . . , she said to herself, absorbed in the counting as she chewed on the chicken.

"What're you doing?" asked Amy.

Startled, Rosemary looked up.

"The way you're eating."

Rosemary was rattled. She hadn't noticed Amy staring at her while she ate. She reached for a subject, any subject but eating. "Who's the guy?" she quickly asked. "The one on the phone this morning?"

Amy grinned. "Special."

"How special?"

"Keep a secret?"

"Sure," promised Rosemary.

"We're getting married."

Rosemary gasped. "Married!" It was as if Amy had slapped her. She was stunned with that same old betrayed and abandoned feeling.

"Help me break it to Mom, will you? I won't be home for Thanksgiving. Christmas either."

"But that's impossible!"

"Mom'll get used to the idea. I'm going skiing with Hank over Thanksgiving. We're going to fly out to meet his folks for Christmas."

Rosemary shoved her plate away and stood up. "You're crazy! The whole thing is ludicrous!"

Amy narrowed her eyes. "Why? What's so terrible?"

Fingers clenched over the edge of the redwood table, Rosemary felt as if she were floundering. She looked out to sea in order to get her bearings. Her eyes followed a flock of toylike sailboats that seemed to be sinking into the horizon. "That guy . . . Hank . . . knows you a few weeks . . . sleeps with you . . . but marriage——"

"Don't say anymore, Rosemary," said Amy evenly.

"What a joke!"

"Shut up, you don't know anything about it!"

"He must be out of his mind!" Rosemary shouted.

"That's enough!"

But Rosemary couldn't be stopped. She glared at her sister's face. It was contorted with pain. No, with guilt. Amy was guilty! "He *has* to marry you! That's it, isn't it? You're pregnant!"

Now Amy stood up, reached over the table, grabbed Rosemary's arm. "Hank doesn't *have* to marry me, he *wants* to! Get that into your stupid little head!"

"Sure he does! Ever take a good look at yourself!"

Amy paled. Shaking with rage, she spoke under her breath. "I've never been the beauty . . . the pampered brat you were. But, at least I'm up-front. People like me for what I am!"

"What exactly are you?" Rosemary spat back at her. "It looks like you're nothing but a slut . . . a common tramp!"

Amy's fingers bit into Rosemary's arm. Then they loosened and she dropped her hand to her side. "And who do you think you are? What have you ever done except sit around looking pretty? I'm sorry for you," she said. "You're a conceited, spoiled, worthless little phony!"

Nine

White-knuckled, Rosemary's hands clutched the wheel of the car, racing it northward.

Amy was despicable! She was a self-righteous, pompous know-it-all!

Turning the argument over and over in her mind, the towns she passed flew by unnoticed. It had always been Amy and Mom against her. Ever since she was very little, she had always been the outcast, she thought to herself. Even now, they invariably spoke to each other over her head, excluding her from their private "woman talk." They still treated her like some kind of doll, only taking her out to play with them when they wanted to be amused.

Tapping her fingers nervously on the wheel, Rosemary drew the car to a halt behind backed-up traffic. The car bucked in starts and stops, hiccuping fitfully, until it picked up cruising speed again.

Still chafing at Amy's words, Rosemary could hear her yet: "What have you ever done . . . sitting around . . . looking pretty . . . conceited . . . worthless."

Well, Rosemary would show her! She'd show them all!

Engrossed in her thoughts, Rosemary realized she was back in the Valley only when some very early holiday decorations on Ventura Boulevard caught her attention. Soon the stores would be crowded with shoppers, the street filled with bumper-to-bumper traffic.

She would get a job! She'd work during the Christmas rush. She'd be independent. She didn't *need* Amy! She didn't need Jason! She didn't need anyone!

When at last Rosemary pulled into her own driveway, a group of well-dressed ladies were just leaving the house after some committee meeting or another. While she waited for the last of them to drive off, she remembered this was the pre-Thanksgiving meeting to arrange for food baskets for the needy. It was one of Mom's favorite projects.

"What a day!" Mom greeted her. "Too much work, too little time." She sat down on the sofa and pulled off her shoes.

Rosemary looked longingly at the leftover cake on the coffee table.

"Want some?" asked Mom.

"Later."

"Oh, Jason came by. Left you a note. It's on the mantle."

"Did he say anything?"

"Just handed me the envelope and took off. Anything wrong?"

Rosemary took the envelope from the mantle and sat down on the hearth. "No. Nothing's wrong."

Mom began emptying the ashtrays.

Opening the envelope, Rosemary thought: He's probably telling me he never wants to see me again. It's all over. Well, I don't care. I don't need Jason anymore.

"Dear Rosemary," she read, "What happened? I can't understand about last night. Let's get together and talk it over. Please. I love you. Jason." There was a postscript: "I'll be waiting for you to call me."

Rosemary's first impulse was to run to her telephone and call him. She wanted to hear his voice. She wanted everything between them to be as it was before. But she couldn't risk it. It had truly turned out exactly the way Trudy had predicted. He had gotten her into bed. He would try it again. The scene in the guesthouse came rushing back to her in vivid detail. His hand on her stomach. His ugly words: "Potbelly . . . dumpling. . . ."

She stuffed the note into her jeans' pocket. Well, he could wait forever before she ever called him again.

"How's Amy?" asked Mom, collecting silverware.

"Fine."

"That's all? Just fine? What's new? Anything going on?"

"Same old things."

Mom sighed. "She may as well be clear across the country, much as I see her. Hardly calls anymore." She laughed ruefully. "Independence!"

Rosemary rankled at the word. "She's got a boyfriend."

"Oh." Mom suddenly looked tired. "I guess that accounts for it."

Rosemary took note of the food remaining around the room. There was a large platter of finger sandwiches beside the cake. On the sideboard was a bowl of ambrosia and a cheese board. Scattered around the room were silver and china dishes of candies, potato chips, nuts. Her hunger jabbed at her.

"Let me clean up. You go rest," she said.

"You're a darling," Mom smiled. "I'll take you up on that."

Rosemary zeroed in on the cake the moment her mother left the room. Without bothering with a plate, she bolted down all that was left on the cake dish. Then she spooned up every remnant of whipped cream still on the platter.

Licking chocolate off her fingers, she carried the dirty plates to the kitchen, put them into the sink, and rushed back to the sideboard. She scooped up a ladle full of ambrosia, stuffed her mouth, then gulped down sweet, leftover fruit punch from the used glass cups. Now she started on the cheese, cracker crumbs falling onto her blouse. Collecting dishes to take to the kitchen, she indiscriminately downed candy, nuts, raisins, potato chips. She hardly broke her stride to gulp lukewarm coffee from the urn on the kitchen counter.

Then, back in the living room, she finished off every sandwich on the tray: ham, cheese, tuna, turkey. Her appetite was insatiable.

Back in the kitchen, she kept the refrigerator door open while she worked. Ice cream. Olives. Bologna. Milk. Roast beef. Sour cream.

She slammed the refrigerator door shut and put the last

remaining cups into the dishwasher. Smiling, she thought: Those early Romans were really on to something. You could binge all you wanted! You could eat your head off! You could stuff yourself up the gazoo! Then all you had to do was throw it all up. Nothing gained. Everything lost!

She started the garbage disposal, then turned to see her mother standing at the stove. She was heating up the tea kettle.

"I can use a cup of tea," Mom said, sitting at the table. "Have some with me."

Rosemary's stomach started churning. She wouldn't have to stick her finger down her throat. She was ready to throw up now.

"What's wrong?" said Mom. "You look sick."

Rosemary felt cold, yet she could feel beads of perspiration on her upper lip. Her hands were clammy. "I'm okay. Upset stomach." She wanted to get away, go upstairs, throw up.

"Sit down," said Mom. "Tea will settle your stomach." She busied herself with the tea things as she talked. "There's a lot of flu going around. You may be coming down with it." She put a cup of tea before Rosemary.

"I don't want any."

"Drink it," Mom said sternly. Looking into Rosemary's face, she sipped her own tea. "You look positively green," she said. "I'm taking your temperature."

Before she could stop her, Mom had gone for the thermometer. Rosemary felt damp. She swallowed wave after wave of nausea.

Mom returned with the thermometer and checked her. "No temperature," she said, with relief. "Finish your tea. Then go up and get under the covers."

Rosemary forced the tea down and got up to leave.

"Leave your door open," Mom said, rising and following her upstairs. "And I want you to call me if you need anything."

In her own room at last, Rosemary took deep gulps of air. She couldn't throw up now. Mom was in her room, right next to the bathroom, and would hear her, become suspicious. But all that food! All that food! She could almost feel it layering into fat! Feel it piling up! She had to do something! But what?

She ran into the bathroom, rifled through the medicine cabinet, found what she wanted. A box of chocolate laxative. Fighting off the nausea, she emptied the contents into her mouth.

Glumly, Rosemary sat in Dr. Feinstein's office. During the night and early morning hours, the laxative had done its work, and there had been no way of preventing Mom from knowing, with all those trips to the bathroom. And there had been no way of stopping her from hauling her off to the doctor today.

Rosemary hadn't attempted to protest. She could handle Dr. Feinstein. She'd known him all her life. She'd tell him about the upset stomach, the diarrhea. She'd tell him she'd eaten a lot of junk food. That would satisfy him.

There was one thing in her favor. The doctor always examined her by herself. Mom would not be in the examining room.

The nurse slid the little glass window open. "Come in, Rosemary," she said.

Rosemary followed Nancy into the examining room. "You know the procedure," the nurse said, handing her a paper gown. "Off with the clothes, on with the latest in Parisian fashion."

Rosemary managed a smile. But when Nancy left and closed the door, she put the gown aside.

"Well, well, well," the doctor boomed as he came in. "What have we here?"

"Hi, doc," Rosemary said, hoping he wouldn't weigh her.

"So, what's the problem?" Dr. Feinstein said, sitting on his swivel stool. "How's the cutest baby I ever delivered?"

"No problem," Rosemary said. "Flu bug, that's all. But you know Mom."

"Yeah." The doctor was eyeing her, but he didn't change his expression. "So let's get Mom off your back, okay?" He unbuttoned Rosemary's blouse, took her blood pressure, and listened to her chest. "Fine," he said. "Now, get on the scales."

As she walked over to the scales, the doctor said, "Dieting?"

"A little," Rosemary said. "Getting ready for the holiday feasts."

Dr. Feinstein weighed her. "Ninety-seven pounds. You can do all the feasting you want."

The doctor didn't seem concerned with her weight, she was glad to see. He waved her to the examining table. "Sit down," he said.

Rosemary watched while Dr. Feinstein studied her file. The worst was over. She was safe. She began to button up her blouse.

The doctor sat down on the stool again and looked at her. "How's it going at school?"

"Great," said Rosemary.

"Still getting all A's?"

"Just about."

"Exercise?"

"Skating. Not too much."

"When was your last period?"

Rosemary hesitated. "I skipped one." She laughed. "Thank goodness."

"Uh, huh." Dr. Feinstein made a note on her chart. He looked up and smiled. "How about boys? Got a steady boyfriend yet?"

"Too busy," said Rosemary hastily. "Carrying a full load at school this semester."

"I see." He flipped through some back sheets in the file.

Rosemary relaxed. The doctor hadn't made a big thing about her diet. She was home free. Or was she? She studied his face. Dr. Feinstein was a man who looked more like an actor than a doctor. His craggy face was lined but still handsome, his white hair rippled with waves. He was always kind, but not patronizing. He was one of the few people she knew who treated her with grown-up respect. He had never talked down to her, even when she was a baby.

"Anything troubling you?" he asked, looking into her eyes.

Rosemary, fumbling with the last button on her blouse, avoided his eyes. "Nothing. Everything's great, couldn't be better."

The doctor stood up, kissed her on the cheek. "I want to see you in my office in a couple of minutes."

When Rosemary came into the office, Dr. Feinstein was sitting at his desk. She took her usual seat in the leather chair.

The doctor was looking down at a book. He ran his hand through his thick hair, then studied her face. Rosemary gripped the arms of the chair.

"Don't look so scared. You're all right."

Rosemary relaxed her grip, leaned back into the chair.

"But you *have* lost too much weight," the doctor went on. "I don't want you to lose any more."

Rosemary stood up to go, but the doctor waved her back into her seat.

"Some kids, girls mostly, get carried away with dieting. It could be serious."

Rosemary squirmed in the chair. She didn't want to hear any more. She didn't need a lecture.

"I want you to be aware of how dangerous excessive dieting can be," said the doctor. He looked down at the book. "It can start innocently. But sometimes it can trigger anorexia nervosa."

"What's that?" she asked cautiously.

"A disease," Dr. Feinstein said. "Becoming more and more common these days." He looked back down at the book. "Let me read you a couple of things about it: 'This illness is most common among the rich, young, beautiful, and female. Chief symptom, severe starvation leading to extreme weight loss.' "

"I haven't got any disease!" Rosemary shot out.

"Just listen, Rosemary," the doctor said calmly. "I'm not saying you have anorexia nervosa, but if you did it wouldn't be a disgrace. Our society practically forces girls to be skinny. The fashion world, television commercials, magazines, movies—they all carry the same message. As if it's some crime to have meat on your bones. As if you can't be loved or respected unless you look like a scarecrow."

Rosemary kept quiet but she felt her anger mounting.

"Maybe it's this liberation thing that makes girls think they're required to be outstanding at something. At any rate, a lot of kids feel pressured into losing more weight than they can afford," the doctor went on. Then he read from the book again. " 'Anorexics do not have poor appetites or no interest in food. The patients are unduly preoccupied with food and eating. But they practice rigid self-denial and discpline to the point of starvation.' " Dr. Feinstein looked up from the book. "Anorexia nervosa can be fatal," he said.

"You examined me. You said I was okay." Rosemary laughed shrilly. "Do I look like I'm dying?"

"Take it easy, Rosemary," said Dr. Feinstein putting down the book. "I've known you from the moment you were born. You've always been a good kid . . . maybe, too good. Part of the problem can come from that. Some kids think that the only way to *really* be their own boss and not just be 'goody-two-shoes' for their families is by controlling their body-weight. It's a way of rebelling against authority. Rebelling is normal. Starving is not."

"Why're you telling me all this?" she said quickly. "My mother's been complaining to you, hasn't she?"

"She's worried, Rosemary. Can't blame her. You *have* lost a lot of weight. I'm concerned, too."

"You don't have to worry about me," she protested. "I'm not one of those nervosa people, or whatever they are."

The doctor came around the desk and sat down on its edge. He took her hand. "You missed your period, honey. That could be a signal, a warning that your body can't handle any more deprivation."

She decided to take a different tack. She withdrew her hand and smiled up at Dr. Feinstein. "I'm sorry I caused you any worry. I'll apologize to Mom, too. I won't lose any more weight, I promise you."

"Good," the doctor said. He went back behind his desk and scribbled a prescription. "I'm giving you some vitamins to stimulate your appetite. And I want some lab tests, so before you leave, see Nancy and she'll help you." He held out the prescription.

Appalled, Rosemary took the prescription from his hand and stood up staring at him.

"And I'll see you in two weeks," Dr. Feinstein said firmly. "To check on your weight."

With almost undisguised fury, Rosemary turned and stormed out of the office.

Ten

Rosemary waited in the car for her mother, who remained behind in Dr. Feinstein's office to hear the results of the examination.

Rosemary, an unreasoning anger smoldering within her, was sure the two of them were conspiring against her. What were they saying? What were they plotting? A sense of impending doom weighted her down, her anger turning to abject, cold fear. What, exactly, was the stuff the doctor had prescribed? Were they *really* vitamins? She pictured a round jug of thick, yellow oil made up of time-released supercalories. And once the globules invaded her body they would go on forever manufacturing great blobs of fat. She would be helpless against it.

She shuddered. As if it were a play, she could picture the interview between her mother and her doctor:

MOM (*melodramatically*): Doctor, what is it? What's wrong with my child?

DOCTOR: Organically, nothing. (*Then ominously:*) *Yet!*

MOM: What can we do?

DOCTOR: I've ordered this medication. A tonic guaranteed to make her fat.

MOM: But will she take it?

DOCTOR: We'll force her. Even if we have to hold her nose and pour it down her throat.

MOM: But will the tonic work?

DOCTOR: (*laughing maliciously*): It will work. It always works. And once it's ab-

GOODBYE, PAPER DOLL

	sorbed into her body, it will continue to work. (*Then, sounding like Vincent Price at his ghoulish worst:*) Traces of it will remain in her body forever. She'll get fat, fatter, fattest! And she'll stay that way!
MOM	(*cackling hideously like a witch*): She'll blow up like a blimp! She'll be like the fat lady of the circus!
SHILL:	Step right up, ladies and gents! See Rosemary, the butterball! Fattest lady alive! Just one quarter, two bits to see the eighth wonder of the world!

Her mother slid in behind the wheel and pulled the car out of the parking lot. Rosemary blinked and brought herself back to reality. Mom's chin was set, a deep vertical furrow in her forehead.

She really didn't want her mother to be worried, yet Rosemary had a sense of elation knowing that Mom was upset about her.

She looked out of the car window as the blocks flashed by. The street decorations sparkled in the warm California sunlight. And she suddenly remembered her plan to find a job.

She reached over and touched her mother's arm. "You know how cautious Doctor Feinstein is. I'm perfectly okay."

"I hope so," Mom said grimly.

"Mom, listen. I'll confess."

"What?"

"I was ashamed to tell you. The reason I got sick is that I scarfed all the party leftovers last night."

Mom looked at her. Then she smiled. Then she chuckled. "Why ashamed?"

"I pigged out. Thought you'd get sore."

Now Mom laughed out loud. "Oh, Rosemary, for heaven's sake! Why didn't you tell Doctor Feinstein?"

"I don't know. Embarrassed, I guess."

"Well, that's a relief," Mom said. She switched on the

radio. The sound of a Christmas carol flooded the car. Mom hummed along with the music.

"Mom?"

"Hmm?"

"I think I'll look for a job."

"Whatever for?"

"Christmas presents. Money to buy gifts."

"I'll call around to the neighbors. They'll be glad you're willing to baby-sit again."

"No, I mean a real job. At a store or something."

"You don't need money that badly," Mom said. "Charge some of the gifts. You've done it before."

"I want to earn my own money for a change."

"But you don't rest enough as it is. Your school work, all the exercise, dating. That's why you're so thin."

"Please, Mom, I'll eat more. I promised the doctor."

"I don't know," Mom hesitated.

"As long as I'm confessing, there's something else. Jason and I . . . we had a fight. I'm not seeing him anymore."

"Oh, I'm sorry," Mom said.

"No sweat," Rosemary said. "But a job would take my mind off schoolwork . . . *and* Jason. I'd get to meet people. It would be fun."

"Your father won't like it."

"It would only be part-time. Just through the holidays. You could fix it with Dad. Mom, please?"

"Maybe it *would* be good for you," Mom said. "Okay, darling, I'll talk to your father."

The car radio continued to play the familiar Christmas music: "Chestnuts roasting on an open fire. . . ."

And Rosemary and her mother sang along. "Merry Christmas to you. . . ."

Rosemary looked at Mom. It felt good to be sitting beside her, enjoying the music. Mom was really okay. A worry wart sometimes, but okay. She wasn't nearly so tough as she made out to be, Rosemary thought. There was a kind of softness and vulnerability about her after all.

GOODBYE, PAPER DOLL 73

Without thinking about it, Rosemary reached over and squeezed her mother's arm. "I love you, Mom," she said.

Her mother's eyes twinkled as she laughed. "You're sort of nice yourself. I think I'll keep you," she answered warmly.

Rosemary felt like a juggler. But she was proud of herself. For the past ten days, she had kept all the balls in the air at once and never dropped one.

The job was a snap. About a mile and a half from home, it was perfect running distance. *Calories lost.*

The job was in a bookstore, which was pleasant and busy. Rosemary handled stock besides waiting on customers. Carrying boxes, filling shelves, wrapping books. *Calories burned.*

She had all her meals under control. She skipped breakfast entirely unless her mother was up. When Mom was watching, she drank her juice and accepted a plate of eggs and a slice of toast. But she'd found a way around eating even that. Hiding a stack of paper napkins in her lap, she surreptitiously pretended to dab at her lips, letting the food fall from her mouth into a napkin. Then, after she finished, she wadded the napkins together in her lap and dumped the whole thing into the garbage compacter on her way out. *No calories consumed.*

Away from home, lunch was no problem. Sometimes she allowed herself a glass of grapefruit juice and an apple; sometimes she had a scoop of cottage cheese and black coffee. But most times, she worked right through the lunch hour at the bookstore. *Calories avoided.*

Dinner was a trial, especially now that Dad was home to stay for the holidays. Everyone else's busy season was her father's slow one, and Mom cooked elegant, gargantuan meals. The napkin routine was out; cloth napkins were used at dinnertime. And both Mom and Dad were closely watching her intake. But, here too, Rosemary kept the ball in the air. She learned ingenious ways to hide vegetables under the meat, to cut and arrange her portions to leave gaping, empty looking spaces on her plate.

And although she had to eat something at the evening

meal, she used all the weapons at her command to counteract the effects of the food afterward. Her dinner over, she jogged down to the empty lot on the corner and vomited among the bushes.

And now she invented a new ritual: she kept some part of her body moving at all times. Sitting, she would swing her legs, rotate her shoulders. Driving, she would practice isometrics, tightening her stomach, her buttocks, as she drove. Trapped in a close situation with her parents, she'd clench and unclench her fists, exercise her feet under the table. Anything to keep moving, to keep active. *Calories worked off, used up, spent*.

Secretly proud of her continuing weight loss, Rosemary began to dress differently so that nobody else would notice and fault her for it. She took to wearing boots to hide her shrinking calves. She bought billowy tent dresses and loose, high-necked, long-sleeved blouses.

But alone at night in her bed, she gloried in running her hands over her prominent ribs, her thin arms, her sharp pelvic bones. Even in bed, she spent hours stretching and doing leg lifts instead of sleeping, wasting her time away. Joyfully, she found that she had to use a pillow between her knees to keep the bones from rubbing together irritatingly while she slept.

The inner Rosemary was now coming forth. She was flat, lean, pure. She was tissue-thin. But she would have to be diligent. She would have to lose even more if she were to win out over her daily doses of Dr. Feinstein's vitamins and her parents' watchful eyes.

In the ten days since she had started to work at the bookstore, Rosemary had lost four pounds.

And now, three days later, her little green notebook contained the entry: *November 17. Seven* A.M. *Weight, 91 lbs.!*

Eleven

Anticipating one of her mother's ridiculous culinary masterpieces, Rosemary was glad to be working at the bookstore on a Sunday. Having gotten away before breakfast that morning, she would burn off as many calories as possible before dinner.

The store was crowded with holiday shoppers. One woman, laden with packages, called out to her. "Miss, do you have something interesting for a boy about ten? He likes horses."

"This way," Rosemary said. Running interference for the woman through the crowd, Rosemary led her to the far end of the store and was already flipping through the pages of a book when the woman reached her.

"This is a popular book," Rosemary said. "The kids love the illustrations."

"Let me see it," the woman said. "I have a whole list of people to buy for. All different ages." She shifted the packages in her arms.

"Let me put your things under the counter," offered Rosemary. "Then we'll take care of the rest of your list."

Smiling broadly, the customer handed Rosemary her bundles. "You're a dear," she said.

While Rosemary dashed to the front of the store to stash the customer's packages, she hoped she could talk the woman into that particular book. It was the last one of its kind on the shelf. That was why Rosemary showed it to her. If the customer bought it, it would mean a trip to the storage room, opening a new carton, and carrying books back to fill in the shelf. Good, thought Rosemary. *Action!*

Taking long strides, Rosemary returned to her customer.

"I can use a book on skiing for a teenager," the woman said, crossing off one of the names on her list.

"There's a terrific one in the sports aisle. It's over here," Rosemary said. Again, she had the book in her hands by the time the woman caught up to her. "Isn't it a beauty?"

"Perfect," the customer beamed. "You really know your stock, don't you?"

Rosemary grinned. She could have shown the lady the same book on the teen shelf in the juvenile department, but this one was on the other side of the store. *Keep moving!*

"Now, I can use a couple of books for my mother and father. They're both into crafts."

The craft section was in the same aisle. "These are nice," suggested Rosemary, "but we have a new shipment in the back. Let me bring a few of the new books out."

"By all means," smiled the woman.

Rosemary hurried to the back room. The carton she was looking for was in a corner behind the juvenile boxes. But she'd bring out only the craft books this time. Save the trip for the children's shelf for later. *Keep going . . . keep busy!*

When Rosemary returned to her customer, the woman had already found two more books she wanted. "You've been so much help," the lady said.

"Thank you," Rosemary said. "If you have any other children to buy for, we have some really nice things back in the juvenile section."

In the children's department once more, Rosemary pointed to the highest shelf. "Those books packaged in series make excellent gifts. Would you like to see them?"

"Sounds wonderful."

Rosemary slid the ladder over and climbed to reach the top shelf. Taking down one package at a time, she made three trips up and down the ladder. *Stretch . . . reach . . . exercise!* As she handed the woman the last package,

GOODBYE, PAPER DOLL

Rosemary hoped the customer wouldn't see the same packaged books on a nearby table.

"These will be fine," said the woman, looking over the books.

"I'll take these to the cashier and give you your other packages," Rosemary said. "Unless you want these gift-wrapped. I'll wrap them if you like."

The woman's smile broadened. "I don't know when I've had such good service. I'd love it, thank you."

Rosemary glowed. Action brought results. Happy customers. *Energy expended!*

Toward the end of the day, Rosemary's zealous activity left her hyper, really wired. But she would not stop. She had skipped lunch, ignored her coffee breaks, and when she went to the bathroom, she had straddled the toilet rather than surrender to fatigue and sit down.

Sorting books, straightening shelves, and displaying gift items between waiting on trade, she worked feverishly, tirelessly.

She was shelving stacks of travel books when she felt a tap on her shoulder. She turned to see someone holding a book in front of his face. The title was *Sex Can Be Funny*.

"Do you need help?" Rosemary said.

"All I can get," answered Jason with a grin as he lowered the book to expose his face. "Got a book called, *Sex and the Single Guy*?"

"Very funny," Rosemary said icily.

"How about, *Everything You Want to Know About Rosemary, but Are Afraid to Ask*? Or maybe you have one entitled, *Great Guesthouse Orgies,* or maybe you stock that bestseller, a sports book named, *Jason Strikes Out*."

Rosemary turned back to the shelf. "If you don't want anything, you'd better leave," she said.

"Oh, I want something, all right," Jason said seriously. "For starters, I want an explanation."

"There's nothing to explain."

"I think there is. Okay, maybe you ran out that night

because you were scared or something. But that doesn't tell me why you won't answer my calls or my notes."

"I'm working. I've been busy."

"That doesn't explain why you run away when I see you at school." He forced her to turn and face him. "Whatever it is, let's talk about it, Rosie."

"I can't . . . there isn't anything to say."

He searched her face for a moment. "You look different," he said, puzzled. "You're sick! You're sick and you don't want to tell me!"

"I'm not sick," she retorted. "Don't you know when you're not wanted? Leave me alone!"

"Rosie, please, let me———"

"Just because a girl won't sleep with you she has to be sick?" she whispered. "You're the one that's———"

"What seems to be the trouble here?" The manager, Mr. Victor, was eyeing Jason suspiciously.

"No trouble," said Rosemary hastily. "He was just leaving."

Jason looked from Rosemary to the manager. Then he wheeled and strode away.

In the back room of the bookstore, Rosemary put her jacket on and was about to leave for the day when the manager motioned her into his little corner office. "I'd like a word with you," he said. He indicated a chair. "Won't you sit down?"

How much had he heard of her conversation with Jason, she wondered. Did he hear the part about sex? Was she going to be fired?

Mr. Victor tamped out his pipe and took a seat behind his small, cluttered desk. "What do you think you're up to?" he said.

Baffled, Rosemary looked at him. "What do you mean?"

Mr. Victor riffled through some papers on his desk. "I've your application here somewhere."

Rosemary apprehensively watched him shuffle the papers around. Mr. Victor sported a beard. He "sported" everything he wore: his pipe, his tweed jacket with leather at the elbows, his very personality. She couldn't decide whether he was imitating a college professor, or an Englishman, or a sophisticated New Yorker, or what. Whatever it was, his clothing and his demeanor looked out of place.

"Ah, here it is," Mr. Victor said, pulling an application from out of the mess. He held the paper at arm's length and squinted at it. "*Rosemary,* correct?"

"Right."

"You've just been here a little more than a week?"

"Yes," Rosemary said. "Anything wrong?"

"On the contrary. You're doing a whale of a job. You don't fancy *my* post, do you?"

"No way," laughed Rosemary with relief.

"Well," said Mr. Victor, "the other clerks are having a time keeping up with you. Patrons are reporting nice things."

"Thanks," smiled Rosemary.

"I've a notion to move you up. How'd you like a cashier's position?"

"Oh, no," Rosemary said quickly. The last thing she wanted was to be sitting at a cash register all day.

"It would fetch you a raise in salary."

"That's okay. I mean, I don't need a lot of money. I enjoy the work."

"But you slave like a bloody coolie. I've had my eye on you."

"I like to keep active. But thanks anyway."

Mr. Victor pulled at his beard and stared at her. "I wish my two sons had half your ambition. Be surprised if they get through prep school at the rate they're going."

Rosemary stood up. "If there's nothing else, I think I'd better go."

Mr. Victor rose and shook her hand. "You're a very attractive little thing," he said. "Look nice at the cashier's station." He held her hand a beat too long.

Rosemary could feel herself blushing. Uneasily, she withdrew her hand. "Good night, Mr. Victor."

"Righto," he said, watching her go.

Twelve

~~~

"You haven't forgotten your appointment with the doctor tomorrow, have you?" Mom said, bringing the rack of lamb to the table and placing it before her husband.

"I canceled it," Rosemary said, trying to sound matter-of-fact. "I thought I told you."

"You didn't tell me." Her mother sat down opposite her father and waited for him to carve the roast.

"Guess I forgot. No, remember in the car, when I told you I wasn't eating because Jason and I broke up? I thought you understood there wasn't any reason for me to go back to the doctor."

"That wasn't my understanding," Mom said. She sighed. "All I see is that you haven't gained any weight. Love is love, but you still have to eat."

"Eat! That's all we do around here! Why does every meal have to be like some damned celebration—candles, flowers, lace tablecloth—why can't we just eat and be done with it?"

"Watch it," her father said warningly.

"We're not animals," Mom said. "I enjoy setting a beautiful table."

"*House Beautiful,*" Rosemary said sarcastically. "Perfection."

Her mother flicked her father a pained look. "That'll be enough, Rosemary," Dad said. He handed Mom a plate and then began carving another rib.

"Just a sliver for me, please," Rosemary said primly.

"I think your mother's right," Dad said, passing her a plate. "You'll keep that appointment."

GOODBYE, PAPER DOLL 81

"All right, all right," said Rosemary grudgingly. "I'll make another appointment for after Thanksgiving."

"Okay," Dad said, smiling. "We'll say no more about it."

She knew she was giving in too easily . . . just as she'd always done . . . all of her life. But if she didn't, Mom would be hurt. Dad would be angry. It was up to her to keep things on an even keel.

She looked from her mother to her father over the candlelight. The candles seemed as bright as torches, the flowers brilliant. The tinkle of silver against china rang like pealing bells in her ears. Her heightened senses pleased her. She was on a special kind of high; like when her parents had let her have too much champagne last New Year's Eve. Colors were intensified, music invaded her very pores; every cell of her body seemed to respond to the slightest stimulus. The raindrops, the clouds, the trees, every leaf took on extraordinary definition. Since losing more weight, she experienced a keenness she had never felt before. Even now, it seemed as if she alone could hear the downpour of the first rain of the season as it pelted the house. She could hear each single raindrop sheeting against the enormous expanse of windows in the dining room.

"Mint jelly?" Mom said.

"Sure, why not?" answered Rosemary. Jelly was one of the easier foods to dispose of. Shove it under the meat and it would melt away.

Careful to leave plenty of meat on the bone, Rosemary then cut the rest of it into quarters. Lamb was one of her favorites, so she gloried in the willpower it took to keep from gobbling it down. She cut one of the quarters into four small pieces, then she began the counting. She would chew each piece twenty-four times. As she chewed, she scooped out part of her baked potato and knifed the scooped-out portion under the lamb bone.

She was so occupied in her camouflage that she hardly even heard the dinnertime conversation. Not until she noticed the angry tone in Mom's voice did she at last look up.

"But I had the whole evening planned!" Mom said.

"Things change. Plans come apart. No disaster. I have to see a client, that's all."

"I see," Mom said. She waited a moment, then: "I'll call the Stacks, tell them we can't make the bridge game."

"Fine," Dad said. "I knew you'd understand."

Mom went to the buffet and brought the chocolate mousse to the table. She *was* a great cook, and her mousse was supreme.

Rosemary took the opportunity to pick up the dinner plates and take them to the kitchen. Mom would never know what was left on her plate. She would deal with the mousse later.

When Rosemary came back into the dining room, Mom and Dad were glaring at each other.

"You don't have to work," Dad said. "I'm quite capable of taking care of my family."

"Financially."

"What's that supposed to mean?"

Mom looked at Rosemary, then purposely refused to answer. "I've been thinking about it for a long time," she said. "I need a job right now."

"Be realistic, you've never had a job in your life."

"To quote you: 'Things change, no disaster.' "

"Don't be ridiculous! What can you do?"

"I'm educated! I can type, do plenty of things!"

Rosemary stood quivering, her fingers grasping the back of her chair. She had never heard a dialogue like this between her mom and dad. There had been many disagreements before, but always polite, refined, on the surface.

"Rosemary's still a kid, she needs you!" Dad said.

Mom's eyes flashed. "It may have escaped your notice, but she's practically grown up!"

Dad scowled. "You don't know the rat race out there! You've had no experience!"

"I'll *get* experience! Even Rosemary has a job! If that *kid* can do it, so can I!"

Her parents glared at each other, for a moment saying nothing. But Mom's words reverberated in Rosemary's ears like crashing cymbals: "... even Rosemary has a *job, ob, ob, ob, ob* ... if that kid can do it, so can *I, I, I, I, I, I*...." Rosemary clapped her hands over her ears, but the sounds sustained: "... so can *I, I, I, I, I*...."

As if on cue, Dad strode out of the house and Mom ran upstairs, both slamming doors simultaneously. Her grip on the back of the chair tightened as Rosemary felt the blows of the doors banging shut, *"bam, am, am, am, am...."* The doors went on slamming inside her head as if she were in an echo chamber.

With effort, she loosened her grip on the chair and walked around to sit down. The three desserts were in front of her. She drew one forward slowly and dipped a finger into it. Like a toothless babe, she licked the mousse off, then dipped her fingers back into it. She tried to think but only jumbled words filled her mind: "I'll huff and I'll puff and I'll blow your house down.... Rosemary has a *job, ob, ob, ob*... she's grown *up, up, up* ... I'll huff and I'll puff and I'll blow your house *down, down, down, down*...."

Scooping up the contents of the second dish of mousse with her fingers, Rosemary enjoyed the sensation of letting the gooey stuff ooze down her throat. Unconcious of the chocolate dripping down her chin, she picked up the dish and, almost in slow motion, licked it clean. The old nursery rhyme sang itself to her: "Jack Sprat could eat no fat,/ His wife could eat no lean,/ And so betwixt them both, you see, /They licked the platter clean."

As she started on the third dish of dessert, Rosemary wiped her chin with her napkin. Mama, mama, she thought. Mama would want her to be *clean, clean, clean, clean*....

"... and pretty maids all in a row...." Daddy liked her to be *pretty, pretty, pretty*....

Pretty! Chocolate mousse! Calories! Fat! Rosemary's only concern now was to undo the damage of the mindless dessert spree she had allowed herself.

She must do penance! She must exercise! She shuddered, suddenly feeling cold. The wind whipped the rain around the corners of the house.

Quietly, so that Mom wouldn't hear, she crept up the stairs to her room. There, she changed into her swimsuit.

Clenching her teeth against the cold, Rosemary went out into the backyard and slipped into the dark swimming pool. The rain beating on her head, she began the punishment for her sin.

Teeth chattering, her skin blue with cold, she finally emerged from the pool. She had done thirty laps.

Now she stood face up to catch the stinging raindrops fully. She was cleansed. She was as a medieval saint. She had sacrificed her hated body to the superiority of her mind.

Thirteen

The note was written in an elegant, distinctive hand. "Rosemary, dear, I hope our friendship does not depend entirely on Jason. Let me know when we can meet for lunch. Fondly, Countess."

When several days went by and Rosemary, not knowing what to do about the note, had not responded, the Countess called her at home. She engaged in no small talk. She simply asked if today was all right, and when Rosemary said it was, the Countess had named the time and place.

She would have to miss school that day, but she didn't care. Having done no homework for more than a week, she was skimming by on luck and past laurels. School had lost interest for her. Her job, her exercise, her preoccupation with food, had left her little time for her studies.

She was dressed in pants and her new full, hand-embroidered smock. All that was left to do was brush her hair. As she stood before the mirror in the bathroom, she admired the shadows under her cheekbones. Cheekbone shadows, a fashion magazine *"Do."* But then she was dismayed to find so much hair left in her brush. Lately, her hair was falling in handfuls, but strangely she had acquired a kind of light peach fuzz all over her body. Dismissing the fuzz as hardly noticeable, she looked at her hair. Dull hair. A fashion magazine *"Don't."* Rosemary sighed. She was certainly as thin as the models in the magazine. But, of course, she needed to be even thinner. She knew herself very well. She knew her penchant for bingeing. As far as her hair was concerned, for the moment she'd pile it up on top of her head. It would look fuller that way, and give her a more sophisticated look as well. She'd think of what to do about its texture another time.

Hair. There was something else about hair that bothered her. What was it? Ah, yes. Mom. Mom hadn't said anything, but Rosemary was sure she was tinting her hair. It was shades lighter than it had been only a month ago. There was something else different about Mom. She seemed to have lost a few pounds, was dressing differently, too. In a way it was kind of funny: Mom, almost in masquerade, trying to look . . . slinky? Trying to look *younger* than she was! Well, a lot of good it would do her, Rosemary thought. Middle-aged and trying to get her first job. What a joke!

Satisfied with her own appearance, Rosemary reaffirmed her image by looking down at her green notebook. *Date, November 19. Time, 8:30 a.m. Weight, 89 lbs.* She had noted it with pride that morning.

Rosemary was shown to her table by the maitre d' of the small but elegant restaurant. It was a garden-like setting, baskets of plants hung from the ceilings, and the booths and tables were separated by lattice and even more greenery. An indoor waterfall, in lieu of music, was conducive to intimate conversation.

The Countess rose when Rosemary came to the table. "How nice to see you again! It's been too long!" She took Rosemary's hand in both of hers.

Rosemary smiled and spontaneously hugged her. But she was rather disappointed that the Countess hadn't mentioned her appearance. If the woman had noticed any physical change, she gave no expression of it.

As Rosemary settled into her chair, the waiter appeared with menus. She turned the pages of the huge menu. There was so much, so much. Everything sounded marvelous. The crepes. The seafood. The soufflés. This was going to be more difficult than she had anticipated.

But then the Countess came to her rescue. She looked up from her menu. "Have whatever you like, my dear.

The food here is divine. I never have anything but a little salad for lunch, myself."

"That's what I'll have, too," Rosemary said.

"The spinach salad is especially nice."

"That'll be fine."

While eating lunch, the Countess carried the conversation with little anecdotes about the dogs, about her cactus garden, about letters from Jason Galanter, Senior. Her eyes shone when she spoke about her son. He'd be home for Christmas. The first time the three of them would have Christmas together in years. Jason was ecstatic, she confided.

And little by little, Rosemary relaxed, enjoying this wonderful woman. Again feeling an affinity with her, a sense of comfort, completely at ease with her.

When the coffee came, the Countess laughed at herself. "But I haven't let you say a word! I hear you have a job at a bookstore."

Rosemary told her about the bookstore and how happy she was to be working, feeling useful.

"Ah, yes," the Countess said. "I can fully understand that." Then dreamily: "There weren't so many options for girls in my day. After the Follies grew tiresome, I was glad to marry the Count. Me, a little Brooklyn girl. He taught me what to wear, which fork to use, how to modulate my voice." She smiled. "But I'm boring you, I'm sure."

"Oh, no," protested Rosemary. "Please go on. I've wanted to hear more about your life ever since we met."

"All right, then. But I warn you I may go on talking forever. Well, the Count was a dear, devoted man." She laughed again. "And he made a lady of me." She fell into a silence while Rosemary impatiently waited for her to go on.

"It took me years to get over his death." She paused. "But then I met Samuel Thomas Galanter and I knew what love could be."

"Jason's grandfather?" Rosemary asked.

The Countess nodded. "We called it the *Grand Passion* in those days. It was the perfect description of a love like that."

"*Grand Passion*," Rosemary whispered.

"So much more fraught with meaning than the contemporary term, *relationship*, don't you think?"

"Oh, yes," Rosemary breathed.

"Knowing Sam was to know love. The joy, the pain, the ecstasy . . . the despair. . . ."

What was Jason's grandfather like? Rosemary wondered. How did the Countess meet him? If the *Grand Passion* was so grand, what made for the pain and the despair? She felt a sharp pang of fear. Was joy and ecstasy worth all that? Intriguing as Samuel Thomas Galanter may have been, the Count sounded much safer.

The Countess reached for Rosemary's hand. "Oh, my dear," she said. "I'm making you feel sad! That wasn't my intention, at all."

Rosemary looked at her bleakly.

"Come, let's stroll in the garden. It's really something to see."

The camellias were splendid in the various colors, from snowy white to variegated to the deepest red. The Countess drew Rosemary into a secluded grotto with a wrought iron bench. Without a word, she nestled Rosemary's head on her shoulder. "It's all right, darling," she said gently. "Whatever it is, it will be all right."

And then Rosemary wept. She sobbed into the woman's shoulder, clinging to her like a small child. And even as she did it, Rosemary knew she was in a safe haven; she was sheltered.

She cried until all that was left was a shudder and an occasional intake of breath.

The Countess embraced her until she was quiet. Then she stroked Rosemary's hair. "You're still so young . . . a baby, really," she cooed. "So fragile . . . so delicate . . . like a little doll . . . a paper doll."

Still holding her in her arms, the Countess went on comforting her. "Dear little Rosemary, I know how afraid you're feeling. I remember . . . no, I won't tell you how scared I was of love when it first came. It was so overwhelming. And I have the feeling you're going through something similar. But it's worth it." She paused, then: "I

GOODBYE, PAPER DOLL 89

just want you to know that I care, that Jason cares. We both love you."

Rosemary straightened and looked into the Countess's eyes. "I know that," she said tremulously. "I know."

"Whenever love comes, it's a precious thing," the Countess said. She noticed Rosemary's surprised expression. "Oh, yes, it can come more than once in a lifetime. But no matter when it comes, it's too precious a thing to throw away. I'm not only pleading for Jason—he'd hate me for that—I'm pleading for both of us. Please don't throw it away!"

And then the Countess did another surprising thing. She got up and left Rosemary sitting alone. And Rosemary was grateful that she had sensed her need to be alone, to have time to pull herself together.

After a few moments, a waiter came bearing a tray of fruit and coffee. "Compliments of Mrs. Galanter," he said and discretely left.

Sipping the coffee, Rosemary began to feel better. She was glad now she had met the Countess for lunch, glad to know that she had someone she could turn to. Some day, she would like to be like the Countess. She too would be sure, knowing, serene.

Sheltered in the little grotto, partially hidden by the camellia bushes, Rosemary still had a view of the stone path winding its way through the garden.

An elderly man carrying a cane stopped to pick a white blossom and put it in his lapel. Rosemary smiled to see his step quicken as he walked on by.

Then a man and woman walking hand-in-hand came past her. They were smiling into each other's eyes, oblivious of the grotto or anything else around them.

With a sharp intake of breath, Rosemary quickly stood up. It couldn't be! It must be somebody else! A lookalike! Of course, it had to be someone else who miraculously looked like him. But then the man spoke and there was no mistaking his familiar voice.

It was her father, all right, and a voluptuous young redhead.

Fourteen

Numbly, Rosemary drove to work from the luncheon with the Countess. She didn't want to think about her father and that woman. What was there to think about actually? It was all so clear, so positively transparent. She was stupid not to have guessed what was going on all along. Surely Amy knew. Everyone in the family was in on the little secret except her! Again, she felt distant and apart and rejected from her family unit.

Luckily, the store was busier than ever and she had no time to think about the situation for the rest of the day. She had her hands full, with two of the employees out sick. She reveled in the work, however, in the running, the stretching, the lifting of cartons, books, packages.

She was the last employee to leave the store that evening and Mr. Victor walked her to her car.

"I must say," he said, as he took her elbow. "You are the liveliest worker I've ever seen. I'd like to propose you to the company as assistant manager of the store."

Rosemary glowed, but at the same time she felt uncomfortable, like a fraud. "No, please. I don't even know how long I can work. My dad isn't exactly pleased at my having a job."

"We'd certainly be sorry to lose you," he said. "Think it over, anyway, won't you?"

"Okay, I'll think it over."

He took her keys from her and helped her get into her car. His hand brushed against her breast as he did so. "Please do," he said smiling.

Rosemary slammed the door and pulled away without saying anything further. Through her rear-view mirror, she could see him still standing there, pulling at his beard thoughtfully, looking after her car.

The house was quiet when Rosemary came in. On the foyer table was a package addressed with her name. On the outside wrapping someone had printed repeatedly: CARE PACKAGE, CARE PACKAGE, CARE PACKAGE, HANDLE WITH CARE, CARE, HANDLE WITH CARE. Breaking the package open, she found a framed photograph of Jason and herself in the tiny pie shop at the beach, looking at each other, she with the smudge on her face. And on the bottom, in Jason's hand, was written: "Because I care. Love, Jason."

Love, Rosemary thought bitterly. What kind of love was Jason offering her? The kind Trudy talked about? The kind where sex was the only thing that mattered?

Or was he talking about the kind of love Hank had given Amy; the kind where love was an obligation, reluctantly given.

Or was Jason talking about the kind of love the Count had offered Jason's grandmother? One in which he could play Henry Higgins to Rosemary's Eliza as in *My Fair Lady*, and attempt to make her into something of his own imagining?

Or was he talking about the kind of love her father was giving that redhead? Or whatever it was he was now giving to Mom?

Then Rosemary remembered the conversation she had had with the Countess this afternoon. Could Jason be talking about the kind of love Samuel Thomas Galanter had given the Countess? Still no good! By the Countess's own admission, that kind of love was filled with pain and anguish. She wanted no part of any kind of love!

She went into the kitchen with the package and its contents. Striding across the floor, she suddenly stopped and held the package close. She turned to go back out. Then she stopped again, changing her mind once more, and hurried back across the room and dumped everything into the trash compacter.

Where was everybody? The table in the dining room

was not yet set for dinner. Mom and Dad were nowhere to be seen.

On her way to her room, she stopped at her mother's door and listened. No sound. She knocked.

"Come in," Mom said. Her mother was in bed, a compress on her forehead. "Sorry, darling, no dinner tonight. Scrounge something up for yourself. I've got a sick headache."

"No trouble, Mom. What about Dad?"

"He won't be home," Mom said. "Called away overnight."

Rosemary's stomach lurched. "Oh." Then: "Can I get you something? Tea?"

Mom shook her head and closed her eyes. Rosemary stared down at her. Pain and anguish, she thought. That's what love is all about. Poor Mom. What could she do for her? She'd do anything to spare her such awful pain. Anything. *Mama, Mama, I love you so much,* she thought. *I wish I could hurt . . . instead of you. I could bear the pain better.*

"Please, Mom, can't I bring you anything, a fresh compress, aspirin?"

"Nothing. I'll sleep it off. I'm just anxious about all that cooking I'm supposed to do for the Thanksgiving baskets."

"Can I start the work on the baskets?" Rosemary asked.

"No, it's all right. Plenty of time to do it tomorrow. You've worked all day."

"Okay, but call if you need me."

Mom turned to the wall. "I'll be fine by morning. Good night."

Left to skip dinner without having to account for it, Rosemary almost missed the subterfuge she was accustomed to indulging in at mealtime.

She was free to swim, to run, to exercise in her room. But she needed something different, anything to keep from thinking.

In the kitchen, she saw four turkeys defrosting. Those would be Mom's contribution for the Thanksgiving baskets. Grocery store sacks were still unpacked. This was the evening Mom had planned to start preparing the dinners to go into the baskets for the needy.

Here was something she could do! She'd surprise her mother by cooking the entire project herself. Rosemary got out the cookbooks and began by planning the dinners from beginning to end. Then she unpacked the sacks and sorted out what she'd need.

In a kind of frenzy, Rosemary started the giblets cooking. Then she began washing and peeling vegetables. She put them in a bowl of cold water until they'd be needed.

She thought of how thrilled Mom would be at saving her all the work as she peeled apples for the pies.

Humming softly as she worked, Rosemary lost track of time. Where she could, she used the microwave oven. Where things needed more space, she used the two conventional, oversized ovens. For the first time in months, she was glad her mother was a conscientious cook and had an extraordinarily modern kitchen.

She enjoyed using the food processor, and all the other conveniences her mother had collected over the years. Rosemary had always liked cooking, but now she took an even greater joy in her activity as she resisted tasting— even once—while she created some of her very favorite foods. Not only the pies, but turkeys, stuffing, gravy, relishes.

When the turkeys began to exude mouth-watering, hunger-provoking scents, she opened the kitchen windows. This would keep her mother from smelling the odors wafting upstairs as well as keep Rosemary from being tempted to eat.

She worked furiously; driven by hunger, she was indefatigable. It was work or think. It occurred to her that another possibility would be to go to bed and sleep, but she rejected that.

She looked around the kitchen with satisfaction. Every available space was taken with good things to eat. Bags of nuts were lined up on the table, plastic tubs of giblet gravy were arrayed on the counters.

At last she was ready to line the ample baskets. Using

the pretty new dish towels Mom had purchased for the purpose, Rosemary placed them so that they would layer the food and serve as covers for the tops. She looked at the pies cooling on their racks, surveyed the browned turkeys set out on the stove top, put the bags of nuts in the bottom of the baskets, and finally sat down at the table to rest. She'd clean the pile-up of dirty pots and pans in the sink later.

"Rosemary!"

Rosemary sat up straight and looked dazedly into her mother's eyes. The woman looked stunned, even horrified. "What—what?" Rosemary stammered. She was groggy, stiff-necked.

"All this!" Mom waved her arms, indicating the results of Rosemary's work. "You've been up all night!"

Rosemary managed a smile. "I wanted to surprise you."

Her mother looked at her in disbelief, then at the enormous display of food. "You surprised me, all right," she said grimly. "Are you out of your mind?"

"What?"

"You've stayed up to do two day's work? What possessed you?"

"You had a . . . I was trying to help." Why was Mom so upset? Why wasn't she pleased? She was only trying to be a good daughter.

"Do you know what time it is?"

Rosemary shook her head, tears springing to her eyes. Why couldn't Mom appreciate what she'd done for her? Why was she mad?

"It's nine-thirty in the morning! You've had no sleep since night before last! Look at you! You look like a refugee from a concentration camp!"

Rosemary looked down at herself. Her apron was drawn tightly over her body. Her sleeves were shoved up above her elbows. When she had kicked off her shoes so Mom wouldn't hear her in the night, Rosemary's pant legs tripped her, so she had rolled them up over her knees.

"Come with me, young lady. I'm putting you to bed and you're staying there for the entire day!"

"But I've got to go to school," she protested.

Her mother looked at her sharply. "No school for you today. And not tomorrow either unless you get some real rest." She took Rosemary by the elbow and led her out of the kitchen. "I don't know what's going on with you, but I don't like it!"

In her room, Mom insisted on helping her undress. Too late, Rosemary tried to stop her. Far too exhausted to argue, she hadn't the strength to oppose her. Down to her panties and bra, Rosemary stood before her mother.

And then her mother took a good look at her, and the secret body she had so carefully been keeping to herself. The incredibly thin body she'd been afraid to expose to both her mother and Dr. Feinstein.

"Oh, my God!" her mother whispered.

Fifteen

Rosemary leaned her head against the back of the car seat. Her mother hadn't wasted a minute in calling Dr. Feinstein for a hurried consultation after seeing Rosemary's naked body.

Still groggy and drunk from lack of sleep, Rosemary just let it happen. She was too tired to care, too exhausted to put up any kind of battle. She dozed for the rest of the drive.

At the doctor's office, Nancy ushered her right into the examining room. This time Nancy undressed her and put her into the paper gown without any joking. It didn't take long for Dr. Feinstein to appear.

"Okay, Rosemary," he said kindly. "Let's see what the damage is." He helped her off the table and led her to the scales. Rosemary held her breath while he fiddled with the weights. "Eighty-eight pounds," he said. "That's nine pounds less than last time."

Now he sounded agitated. "Did you hear anything I told you when you were here last?"

Rosemary nodded. "I heard."

"But you chose not to listen? You want to look like this? You want to feel like this?" he asked, putting her back on the examining table.

"I look okay. I feel good," Rosemary mumbled.

"I can see that," said Dr. Feinstein. "Can you tell me why you're doing it?" he said while he took her blood pressure.

"You don't have to be so mad," Rosemary said, surprised at her own angry retort.

"Yes, I do," the doctor said. "I bring a perfectly

healthy kid into this world, do my best to keep her that way, and what does she do? Ruins her body for the sake of fashion! Why?"

Rosemary, refusing to answer, looked up at him sullenly.

"Answer me!"

"You're the doctor! You tell me!" she said sarcastically.

The doctor made a note of her blood pressure, sat on his stool and looked at her. "You're right," he said in a defeated tone. "I *should* be telling you." He shook his head as she sat up. "But there isn't much I can tell you. Your lab tests were okay, but still . . . there isn't much we know about this disease."

"What disease?"

"Then you didn't hear anything I told you last time. All right. I'll tell you again." He looked to make sure she was listening. "Anorexia nervosa. It's a disease. You've got it."

Rosemary remembered something about that dumb thing from the last time. She started off the table.

"You sit right there!" Dr. Feinstein ordered. "You're going to sit there until I know you've heard me!" He shifted in his seat, took a breath, and began again. This time in the fatherly tone Rosemary was used to: "You're still dieting, aren't you?"

Rosemary shrugged. "Not entirely."

"Then you're eating and throwing up after, right?"

"How do you know that?"

Now, the doctor imitated Rosemary's shrug. "I can't prove it, can I? So you're eating, then vomiting. Also taking laxatives. Also exercising until you drop. Also not sleeping. Hair falling from your head but growing on your body. Do I have it all, or have you got any more surprises for me?"

Now Rosemary grew frightened. It was as if the doctor had invisible spies watching her every moment of the day and night. If he knew all that, he would also know how to make her gain weight, make her fat! She clutched the paper gown around her.

"Listen, darling, I'm not your enemy. I want to help you. I'm not scolding a dumb kid. I'm advising a smart one." He came to the table and tilted her chin so she'd have to look into his eyes. "I'll do what I can medically, but that's not enough."

Rosemary fought back tears. When the doctor was angry, she could fight him, but when he was tender with her, her weapons of combat failed.

"I'm not a psychiatrist," the doctor said.

Rosemary stiffened. She was about to speak when he put his fingers over her lips.

"You're not crazy. Nothing like that. It might be a problem in wanting to grow up and, at the same time, *not* wanting to grow up. That's common enough."

Rosemary turned her face from him.

"It's no disgrace, Rosemary. It's a push-pull thing. Sometimes it's frightening to grow up."

"I'm not afraid. I *am* grown up. I have a job. . . ."

The doctor sat back down on his stool. "I'm not arguing with you. I'm *telling* you. This dieting . . . it's more than being skinny or fat. It's a very serious medical matter. Also, a psychological problem. You'll have to see a psychiatrist."

"Supposing I won't go?"

The doctor looked at her squarely. "If there's no improvement in your condition—and soon—I'm going to put you in the hospital. It's up to you."

"Hospital! What for?"

"To keep you alive. To keep you from starving yourself to death."

Mother and daughter were silent driving back home in the car. Rosemary was scared. She had never been so scared in her life.

One thing she knew, she wasn't going to any hospital. They weren't going to ruin everything she'd fought so hard to attain. In the hospital she'd be at their mercy. They could force anything and everything into her. The hospital was out!

The psychiatrist was her only hope. From what Rosemary had heard and read about psychiatrists, all they ever did was talk. She could handle that. Talk was safer. Frightening, too, but safer. There were no calories in conversation.

It's up to you, Rosemary, Dr. Feinstein had said again in his office in front of Mom. *Think it over.*

It was up to her! If it were really up to her, she'd tell them both where to go. She wasn't the one who was complaining. She was perfectly content to go on the way she had been.

She shot her mother an angry look. If Rosemary hadn't wanted to please her, surprise her with fixing the Thanksgiving dinners, none of this would have happened. From now on, she'd think of nobody but herself. She'd have to be wary, cunning. She could easily outfox her mother, and she'd find a way to get around the psychiatrist—if she couldn't find a way to keep from going altogether.

Mom watched while Rosemary drained a glass of warm milk and honey. Then she tucked the covers up to Rosemary's chin, drew the shades, and told her to sleep as long as she wanted.

As soon as Mom left the room, Rosemary tried to get up to get rid of the milk. But she couldn't move. It was as if her arms and legs were anchored with heavy rocks. She closed her eyes and fell into a restless sleep:

She was driving her car up a steep incline. It was so steep, it seemed as if—should she reach the top—she would drive off into nothingness. She clenched the steering wheel and gave the car more gas. But the wheels spun crazily; the car only inched upward.

She had to get up to the top; her life depended on it. Arrows pointed straight ahead. "No U-Turn," signs proclaimed. But the more she accelerated, the more she seemed to be slipping back. She gave the car a burst of gas. Now it began to climb slowly and she could hear a strange sound as the wheels turned. There was a sticky substance on the road. It clung to the wheels like hot tar, making the ascent even more agonizingly slow. She was nearing the summit. Her heart pounded painfully in her chest. Would she fall off into a void? Would the road run smoothly down the other side?

The sticky substance disappeared and in its place was slick ice. The wheels lost traction and the car backed down, dizzily swerving from one side of the perpendicular road to the other.

A traffic officer appeared at the window of the car. He wanted to see her driver's license. Rosemary was panicked. He was threatening to take her to jail.

Rosemary searched her glove compartment. There was no license there. She looked under the seat of the car. The black-suited officer pulled out his handcuffs.

Then she noticed a large, brown leather bag on the seat beside her. She felt relieved. The license would be in it. In her wallet. She put her hand into the bag.

Shocked, she felt her fingers squish something warm and mushy. Pulling out her hand, she saw chocolate pudding all over it, dripping globs of it into her lap. The officer laughed and slipped a handcuff over her wrist.

Then she looked up and saw water spilling down from the top of the hill. The water trickled at first, then rushed, then cascaded, then the entire hill became a torrent. Now, a tidal wave taller than the incline, itself, hovered over her. It hesitated at its crest, seemed to take a deep breath, then it crashed down . . . down . . . down . . . engulfing her . . . drowning her . . . she gasped for breath . . . there was no air . . . she was thrashing around in the water . . . air . . . air. . . .

Rosemary sat straight up. Her body was drenched with sweat, her hair matted and wet. She looked up. No tidal wave. A dream. A nightmare. Darkness edged the window shades. She licked her lips. Dry. She had to have a drink of water. She felt sticky. She smelled of hot tar. She needed to get clean!

In the shower, Rosemary used her back brush all over her body. She shampooed her hair, then started the procedure all over again.

GOODBYE, PAPER DOLL 101

Wrapped in a towel, she scrubbed her teeth until her gums bled. Then she dusted herself all over with bath powder.

Opening her closet door, she looked at her image in the mirror. Good. Flat stomach. Hardly any curve of breasts. Pointed elbows. Prominent clavicle bones.

She turned. The gross, vulgar demands of her body had been happily denied. Little, sharp wings stood out under her shoulders. Her rear was sleekly trim. Her body was cleanly powdered.

For a moment, Mom's solemn face and Dr. Feinstein's angry one crossed her mind. They were against her. They were all against her. Mom, Dad, Dr. Feinstein . . . and soon some weird psychiatrist. She'd have to defy them all. She'd have to stand off all of them.

But then she smiled. She suddenly felt in complete control. Powerful!

She studied the stretched skin over her facial bones. She'd be like that from head to toe, taut, sharp. She'd be ready for them. Now, she would diet in earnest! They couldn't stop her!

Sixteen

Ta-ta-ta-boom! Ta-ta-ta-boom! The big, bass drums went by followed by half a dozen boys, dressed in cowboy suits, on buckskin ponies.

Rosemary surveyed the noisy, excited crowd lining the street. Little kids were sitting in the gutters on blankets, pillows, newspapers. Others were on the curbs sitting at the feet of their parents. Some had prime seats on the shoulders of their dads and older brothers.

After the ponies there was space, and then the streetwide banner of Grant High School, held up by the banner girls, went by. The people roared their approval. Now the drum major, decked out in snowy-white and wearing an enormously tall, plumed shako, high-nosed by. He was followed closely by the briefly dressed baton twirlers in the blue-and-white Grant High colors. Stacy and a couple of her sidekicks grinned at the catcalls and shrill whistles their appearance provoked from guys in the crowd.

What a crock, Rosemary thought. With their fat, dimpled knees, their grossly rounded behinds, they were like overpadded cows. But there was something different about Stacy. She was thinner than the rest, noticeably more slender.

The band music quickly drowned out the sound of the hecklers. Rosemary didn't quite know why she was here. Perhaps it was because she couldn't remember a single Thanksgiving Day when she hadn't viewed the annual parade down Van Nuys Boulevard. She remembered when she too had proudly occupied that lofty position on her father's shoulders.

GOODBYE, PAPER DOLL

The Van Nuys Thanksgiving Day Parade was, at best, a poor imitation of the famous, showy Hollywood Lane Parade which was held later in the evening, but it couldn't be beaten for the enthusiasm of both the viewers and participants.

Rosemary's late afternoon Thanksgiving dinner had been a bleak, uncomfortable one with Mom and Dad barely speaking. When they talked to her, it was with an artificial deference to her illness. But the anger it covered was apparent enough. And she felt anger in return. It wasn't she who had pronounced herself sick, was it?

Half-heartedly mentioning the parade, Mom said she was too tired to go, and Dad said he was going to watch football on television. So Rosemary had elected to go to the parade by herself. Anything to get out of the gloomy atmosphere of the house.

Now the dark-suited band teacher walked beside the band while it filed by. The flutes and piccolos pierced Rosemary's ears painfully, and she was glad when the woodwinds followed. She recognized some of her classmates playing clarinets, saxophones, bassoons.

Assaulted by the blaring brass section, Rosemary became aware of a headache starting over one eye. Unconsciously, she moved back as the trumpet and trombone players, cheeks puffing, stepped past.

Her eyes held on the xylophone player; his mallets were a blur over the bars of the instrument slung around his neck.

With the crash of cymbals, the pain over her eye began to throb earnestly. Rosemary pressed her fingers to her temples as she watched the tenor drums, the marching snares, and the bass drums go lumbering by, noisily beating out the step. The tuba, its opening covered with a transparency emblazoning the school letters, oompahed importantly.

And now came the beautiful, even-gaited Peruvian Passos, ridden by men in long, flowing white ponchos. Clanking with heavy, silver-encrusted saddles and bridles, another equestrian group rode by, and then a blur of color as clowns, antique cars, dancing American Indians, Mexican mariachi bands, and elaborately headdressed red-skinned men on spotted-butt Appaloosas followed one after another.

Between other high school bands, local politicians rode in Pierce-Arrows and Model-T's. And floats of every description, carrying Stacy-like girls with long, yellow hair, wheeled past.

Little known starlets and has-been movie stars waved enthusiastically from atop cars and floats. Streamers and confetti filled the air as the last of the bands brought up the rear of the parade.

Rosemary was one of the first to make her way out of the crowd. Her car was parked at the Sherman Oaks Park, but she was reluctant to go back to the hostility she might find at home.

She sat on the grass in the park, leaning against a tree. From a distance, she could see a small group of girls straggling closer. Some were in costume, a few in street dress. Rosemary recognized Stacy, Trudy, and some of the others.

"Hey, Rosemary! Rosemary Norton!" Stacy called. Twirling her baton, she high-stepped it over to the tree and sat down next to Rosemary.

"Hi, Stacy." Rosemary drew up her knees and sat up straight against the tree. She looked at Stacy. Stacy must have lost ten, maybe twelve pounds. And even sitting, there was something vibrant about her. She was like one of those highly bred horses in the parade.

Trudy, eating a foot-long hotdog, flopped down on Rosemary's other side. "Hi, pal," she said.

Rosemary nodded. The two hadn't spoken since that day of the fight in the cafeteria. Was this some kind of ruse, or did Trudy really want to make up?

One of the other girls, her face hidden by a cone of spun sugar, shuffled up to them. Three other girls, carrying popcorn and ice cream cones, followed. "Hey, lookit the swings!" said the spun-sugar girl. "Come on, gang!" Giggling and yelling, the girls ran off toward the play area.

"How've you been?" Stacy said. She looked at Rosemary.

"Fine," said Rosemary stiffening. "Wonderful."

"Miss Pickett has been asking about you," Stacy said.

"I know." Rosemary had found a note from the gym teacher pinned to her locker a couple of weeks ago. It asked that Rosemary report to the school nurse. Rosemary had ignored the note and skipped gym from that day on. When she had been called to the nurse's office, Rosemary assured the nurse she would be getting a note from the doctor excusing her from taking phys-ed. So far, the nurse had not called her on it.

"I don't need P.E." Rosemary said.

"I envy you," Stacy said suddenly. "I really do. There's no one around that's got as much stamina as you have."

Trudy coughed, her hotdog held halfway to her mouth. "I think I'm missing something," she said when she caught her breath. "It takes stamina to starve?"

"You wouldn't know anything about it," Stacy said in a superior tone. "Tell me," she said to Rosemary. "Do you use those water pills?"

"Water pills!" Rosemary scoffed. "That's not true weight loss. That's just dehydration."

"You two can't be for real!" Trudy exclaimed.

"Shut up and eat!" Stacy said tartly. "Listen, Rosemary, how do you lose a lot of weight . . . I mean a lot in the shortest time?"

Rosemary relaxed against the tree. The sharp pain in her head only seemed to make her more alert. "How much do you weigh?"

"Ninety-seven," Stacy said. She flushed, seeming ashamed of the number.

"That's not so bad. You're tall. Five-seven, at least, aren't you?"

"Yeah, but you're almost as tall as I am and twice as thin."

"I don't believe it!" Trudy said. "Listen, Rosemary, she's putting you on. Everybody knows you're too skinny . . . like a skeleton . . . She's just——"

"I told you to butt out," Stacy said harshly. Then to

Rosemary: "I think you're terrific, I mean it. I'm sick of being one of the mold. I want to be different. Like you. Have the courage to create my own kind of lifestyle. I don't want to be a dumb float queen for the rest of my life."

Rosemary couldn't believe her own ears. "But you're beautiful! I'm the one who was always jealous of you!"

"You know you're the talk of the school. Come on, what's your secret?"

Part of Rosemary was beginning to really enjoy the conversation, but another part was becoming perplexed, confused. "Nothing mysterious about it," she said. "I just eat a little less each day than I ate the day before."

"No special diet?"

Rosemary shook her head. "Just a constant one. And continuous exercise."

"What about your parents? Aren't they wild? I know, mine are. And I've hardly lost any weight at all."

Rosemary shrugged. "I can handle them." Then it was she who began to question: Why would the most popular girl at school want to change that? Stacy was a beauty, didn't she know it? She was always the center of attention. Wasn't that gratifying?

While Trudy looked on open-mouthed, Stacy confided in Rosemary. She mostly felt like a total turn-off, with no attributes other than her appearance. She needed to know what she could do, how far she could stretch. Having dates, being popular, that wasn't where it was. That was petty stuff—didn't make her feel *real*. She needed to know what she was basically made of . . . deep down.

Finally, Trudy interrupted angrily. "You listen to me, Rosemary. I don't know what kind of game Stacy is playing, but *it is* a game! She's jealous of all the talk about you! Can't stand the attention taken away from herself! Don't listen to her!"

Then Trudy turned on Stacy: "You don't care who you hurt, do you? Just as long as you get all the attention! It may be some kind of weird game to you, but it isn't to Rosemary! Can't you see that? You want to see her die? You want to help kill her?"

GOODBYE, PAPER DOLL

Stacy let fly a hard slap to Trudy's face. "Bitch!" she exclaimed.

Trudy's head snapped back with the impact. Her hand forming a fist, Trudy drew it back. For a moment, Rosemary thought there would be an out-and-out fight.

"I'm glad you did that! Showed your bared fangs!" Trudy said through clenched teeth. She stood up and appealed to Rosemary: "She's using you! Can't you see it? I wouldn't lie to you! I never have!"

"You don't have to defend me. I don't need your help," Rosemary said quietly. Then she turned her face and walked away.

Driving home, Rosemary could feel the pulse at her temples pounding harder and harder. She was sick to her stomach, but stronger feelings surfaced, overwhelmed her. There was pride, satisfaction, gratification; and there was also uneasiness, dread.

Stacy. She couldn't take her mind off the phenomenal conversation they had had. Stacy, with her following of guys and girls, the princess of the school, had come to her for advice. Stacy was jealous of *her!*

But Stacy would never make it, Rosemary thought. Stacy would never be able to detach herself from her familiar role. She was too self-centered, too weak. She would never be known for anything other than her looks. She did not have the fortitude required.

Rosemary had the reputation of something more substantial, more important than mere looks. She was head and shoulders above any "pretty" girl. Like Joan of Arc, she had courage. Like Madame Curie, she had tenacity. There was purpose, direction to her life. She had accomplished drastic changes in her very personality.

It didn't matter whether or not Stacy was playing a game. Rosemary knew her own life was far from frivolous. It was mature and thoughtful. It was dedicated. She had shed herself of the repugnance of pettiness and childishness. She was independent of the opinions of her classmates, of the grown-ups in her life . . . or was she?

It was hard to remember the girl she used to be. The

things that were important to her: clothes, being cool, popular. What a phony she had been!

What was important now was purity, purity of body and spirit. She was driven by self-sacrifice, relentless in her search for independence. There was no acting, no performance in her behavior, and she would do better still. She would drive herself to the very limit and not be found wanting.

The struggle, the pain, would be well worth it. Rosemary let her headache take over. She could take the pain; she welcomed the pain; she revelled in it! Bring on the punishment! There was nothing she could not withstand! She was prepared to punish herself and endure!

Seventeen

Having started her new, intensified regimen, Rosemary jogged all the way to work on Monday. The weather was damp and cloudy, a penetrating cold chilling her through her thin blouse. Disdaining her heavy sweaters and jackets, Rosemary chose to bear the cold rather than buckle under.

The bookstore was filled with shoppers seriously bent on getting their Christmas gift buying out of the way now that Thanksgiving had officially heralded the holiday season.

Rosemary tried to keep her mind on her work and away from thoughts of Jason. But however much she tried, she couldn't help thinking of him now and then.

Only this morning, she had heard from him. This time, it was in the form of a Christmas wreath she found on the visor of her car windshield. A note attached read: "My Dad's coming in for the holidays. Spend Christmas Eve with us? Love, Jason."

It didn't seem to matter whether she answered his messages or not; they still kept coming. The day before Thanksgiving she had received a white chocolate turkey with the message:"Stop being such a turkey. Call me!" And a few days before that, she'd had a real, live singing telegram. The girl who delivered it had been outfitted in a page boy costume and had brought along her own tap dancing board. She sang a Thanksgiving Day version of *Happy Birthday to You*, and buck-and-winged until Rosemary had tersely asked her to leave.

And at school today, Rosemary had found pinned to

her locker a picture of Jason making a grotesque face. On the bottom was written: "Can't you love a face like this?"

Jason was not an easy guy to dismiss.

Most unusual for her, Rosemary did take a coffee break while at work. Sitting in an Orange Julius booth, she slipped off her shoes and rubbed the soles of her feet. With practically no padding on the bottoms, her feet were hurting furiously under the strain of jogging and working. She sighed. She could take it. This was only another opportunity for her to prove herself. She accepted the hurting feet as she had accepted Thursday's headache and every day's hunger pangs, with a perverse kind of pleasure. She sipped at her black coffee and wondered what the mindless people around her would think if they knew what she was really going through.

After she finished her coffee she still had a few minutes left, so she went into the penny arcade next door. There was an old-fashioned fortune scale she liked to weigh herself on from time to time. She slipped her penny into the slot and withdrew the ticket from the scoop below. "A good time to begin new ventures." She took this as an omen portending more successful weight loss now that she had begun her new and rigorous phase of dieting. Her weight: eighty-six pounds.

She'd had nothing for breakfast. Fine. She had jogged around the track at school during lunchtime. She did have something during snack break. She had decided to buy only what she loved best from now on, but only eat a tiny bit of it. So she had bought her favorite—a great hunk of chocolate cake. She had filled the cavity of a teaspoon with some of the cake, thrown the rest away, then spent the entire twenty-minute break licking at the spoon. Delicious! And weight watching!

Thinking of the teaspoon of calories she had consumed, Rosemary spent the rest of her working hours at the bookstore in frenzied activity. And again, she was one of the last employees to leave.

Crossing the parking lot, Mr. Victor called out to her. He was standing beside his car. "Rosemary! Here!"

Rosemary hobbled over to him. Her feet were hurting

dreadfully. She would have to give in and soak them for a while when she got home.

"No coat?" Mr. Victor asked. "You'll catch your death. It's a beastly evening!"

"I'm not cold," Rosemary shivered. "Jogging warms me up."

"Oh, come now! You're not going to jog home! I won't hear of it!"

"I don't mind. I like it."

Mr. Victor opened the car door and handed her inside. "Nonsense," he said as he placed a hand on her shoulder. "I'll see you home. I won't hear otherwise."

He slammed the door and walked to the driver's side. Sliding in, he said, "I've yet to see anyone as active as you. You'll wear yourself to a frazzle if we're not careful."

Rosemary sighed. She would rather have walked. But she had to admit to herself that she felt better sitting down. She let herself indulge in the pleasure. She leaned back in the seat, closed her eyes, and waited for the hum of the engine.

Then, suddenly, Mr. Victor was upon her. Holding her tightly, he kissed her full on the lips, his tongue reaching for hers.

She pushed at his shoulders, but he held her even more tightly. He was breathing heavily, his beard scratching her neck. "Come on, baby," he was saying. "Give a little. What do you say?"

She turned her face from his. "Let me go!"

"Don't be that way, little girl," he said. He loosened his grasp and let his hands slide down over her chest.

"Let go of me! Let me out of here!"

Mr. Victor's hands found their way under her full blouse, reached between her breasts. "Relax, baby."

Given that much space, Rosemary pushed him with both her hands, then quickly grasped the door handle and let herself out. As soon as her feet hit the ground she began to run. Dodging between parked cars, she raced through the lot. She forgot her painful feet, forgot her exhaustion.

Without looking over her shoulder, without stopping to see if Mr. Victor was chasing her or not, Rosemary ran block after block until she turned into her own street.

At her door at last, Rosemary pulled her keys out of her jeans' pocket. Her throat was dry, her breath came in rasping pants. Trembling, she held the key to the lock. Then, as if a dark shade was passing before her, she felt the blackness engulf her. Falling against the door, she heard the crack of her head against wood. And then—nothing.

She was in her own bed and Dr. Feinstein was looking down at her. She turned her head. Mom and Dad were standing on the other side of the bed.

Rosemary sat up straight. "Gotta run! Gotta go!"

The doctor cradled her in his arms. "No more running," he said. "You're home. You're safe."

Lying back down on her pillow, Rosemary gazed up at her parents. Her mother was crying. Her father looked worried. "You trying to kill yourself?" he said.

"That can't help," said the doctor. He looked at Rosemary. "I'm putting you in the hospital. You'll stay there until you're better. A few days, maybe."

"No! I won't go!" Rosemary cried.

"Can't we take care of her at home?" Mom asked.

"Too dangerous. Pressure's too low." The doctor turned to Rosemary. He smiled at her. "While you were so busy sleeping it off, I got in touch with a friend of mine. Doctor Lillian Collens. She'll be in charge while you're in the hospital."

"I don't want to go! I'll eat! I promise!"

"You'll be admitted tonight." He looked at her parents. "Bring her to Valley Community in about an hour. I'll see about getting her a bed."

Rosemary began to cry. "Please, doctor."

"I'm sorry, Rosemary. But you could go into shock. You're almost there already." He took her hand. "It's not so terrible. All we'll do is save your life." He laughed at his own joke. Then, seriously, he said: "Rosemary, it's up to you. If you do eat, like you say you will, you can walk out under your own steam in a few days. Gain several pounds, that's all I ask. But if you don't improve, we'll have to feed you forcibly."

"Forcibly!" Mom gasped.

"Intravenous. It's nothing." Again, he looked at Rosemary. "I'm not punishing you, honey. It's only a precautionary measure. For your own safety."

He kissed her wet cheek. "I'll see you over there. Introduce you to my friend Lillian. Settle you in. You'll have a good rest. Like at a hotel." Then to the parents: "About an hour, okay?"

Rosemary heard the snick of a luggage latch. Staring at the ceiling, she knew without looking that Mom had packed up a bag for her to take to the hospital.

She would not go to the hospital. She would not. She would think of something. She was good at coming up with ideas to circumvent older people.

But she was feeling drowsy. Dr. Feinstein had injected her with something. As soon as Mom left the room, she would get up and have a cold shower, wake herself up. She would not sleep. If they took her to the hospital, they'd have to take her kicking and screaming. They'd have to take her by force.

Mom shut the door when she left the room. Rosemary kept her eyes wide open. Still staring at the ceiling, she could hear her parents downstairs. They were probably planning her departure. They were, no doubt, glad to see her go. Well, she'd put up a real fight. They'd have to force her . . . force her . . . force her. . . . Her eyes snapped shut. Mouth open, head lolling to the side, she breathed in a heavy, drugged sleep.

She was on a conveyor belt moving down an endless, white space. Her mouth, with a large metal funnel suspended over it, was propped open with wooden tongue depressors. Her arms and legs were tied down with leather straps. And rubber tubes of various sizes had been inserted into her limbs. As she gawked with horror at the ceil-

ing above her, she could see tangles of translucent pipes feeding thick, mucus-like calories into the tubes.

As the conveyor belt moved her slowly along, great, disembodied balloon faces leered down at her. The white balloon was Dr. Feinstein. It hovered over her, floating along, grinning hideously. Then it was replaced by a blob, Mom's pink face, her cheeks puffed out grotesquely. A thick, black furrow ran down the center of her forehead, blood-red tears streamed down her face. Above the pink one, two more balloons with strings intertwined, playfully bounced off each other. One was yellow, the face of that redhead, the other, brown, with Dad's features painted in a kind of a happy-face.

Now she passed under a bunch of balloons held by Jason, the balloon man at the Thanksgiving Day Parade. What was he doing at the hospital? The balloons he held were the green face of Trudy, the royal blue one of Amy, the murky orange one of Mr. Victor.

Rosemary strained at her leashes, but could not release herself. The balloons rode the air above her as the funnel continued to drip oily, oozy stuff down her throat. She wanted to throw up, but lying on her back it was impossible.

Now, the conveyor belt began to tilt upward. As she rose, feet first, she could see only her toes. She knew the end of the belt was coming and she'd be plunged into a deep vat of gurgling, thick, syrupy stuff.

Up, up, up she went and the balloons began to laugh crazily. She wanted to scream, but nothing came forth. The gurgling sound rose, filling the air with the plop of burst bubbles: blup . . . blup . . . blup . . . ba-looop. The stench of molasses filled the heavy air.

And now, she was at the top, now over the top, now falling, falling, falling, falling. . . .

Dad's voice boomed from downstairs: "I didn't know I'd be falling for her!"

"Falling!" shouted Mom. "So busy falling for that whore, you couldn't see how sick your own daughter was! I tried to tell you . . . tried to talk——"

"You never talked to me! You talked *at* me! Don't lay Rosemary's sickness on me! You work so hard to make our marriage look ideal, you've refused to face what it really is!"

"Since when is protecting my kids from ugliness a crime!" Mom screamed. "Showing them the better side of life?"

"What better side of life? How about real life? You and your illusions! Every time I opened my mouth to suggest something, you told me it was love . . . or her age . . . a phase . . . anything to get off the hook yourself!"

As if still in her dreams, Rosemary rose from her bed. She slipped on her jeans and a sweatshirt. Putting on her socks and shoes, she had to tie and retie the laces. Her coordination was off. Something the doctor had injected her with. Her head felt light, disconnected from her body. There seemed to be large spaces of time in between as she went into the bathroom to wash her face, towel it dry, walk back into the bedroom—spaces of time unaccounted for.

She floated down the stairs soundlessly. Passing the living room, she heard her parents' voices screeching and tumbling over each other.

Mom was sobbing. "I did the best I could. A man takes up with some slut young enough to be his daughter! What did you expect me to do? Carry on like a fishwife? You'd have liked that, wouldn't you?"

"I'd have liked you to care!"

"Care! Care! *I've* instilled good values into our girls! I thought you'd get over this middle-aged . . . whatever it is! I thought you'd come to your senses!"

Unseen by Mom and Dad, Rosemary padded into the kitchen.

"Cover-up! You're so good at cover-up, you ought to go into politics!" yelled Dad.

"And you're so good at flashing money around . . . living it up . . . girls . . . trips . . . gambling . . . you ought to go into show business or something!"

"God damn it! What're you talking about? A man's got

a right to enjoy what he's earned! I'm not self-sacrificing ... a martyr...."

Rosemary opened the back door and walked out to the driveway. She got into her car and let it roll down into the street.

She started the engine and gunned the motor. Pulling away from the house, she smiled, and drove off into the night.

GOODBYE, PAPER DOLL

As if to make up for its mischief, the fog lifted enough to let the one light of the car lead it downward, past looming eucalyptus trees, high block walls, a hook in the road, private gates, curly-tailed road signs.

Then a green arrow blinked left, left, left, left. Ah, a straight road again. Where did it lead? Spaces. Boundless spaces, leading to infinity. The ocean at her right, Rosemary wove down the Coast Highway, in and out of pockets of fog.

Sheer, creviced cliffs appeared on the left, houses perched precariously at the edges. Watch for falling houses. Flares flickered around a landslide area. "I'll huff and I'll puff and I'll blow your house down." Spaces. Windy, dangerous spaces.

Santa Monica. The Fish Shanty at the foot of the pier. Free parking. Plenty of parking space. Plenty of spaces. Spaces. She parked behind a store on the pier.

Roar of ocean. Bottomless ocean of space. And spaces. The pier. Skate. Get the roller skates from the trunk of the car, she thought. She put on the skates. She tied and retied the laces. Her coordination was mixed up. Something the doctor had injected her with. Spaces.

She rolled, as if wafting on a breeze, across the parking lot. Another parked car. She slowed down. Looked into the window. Arms, trunks, legs intertwined like wriggling worms. She watched, fascinated. The appendages separated, became figures. Voices: "Get away from here! Weirdo!" Spaces. The car door opened. A male figure pushed her. She rolled away on her skates. Spaces. She covered spaces.

She went past the ancient merry-go-round. Dark shadows of horses paraded forever in a circle. Going nowhere. Stepping to the beat of the silent calliope. A futile race. Their world moved. They were nailed into their spaces.

The ocean on both sides of the pier, she drifted on her skates. No effort. The fog thickened. Patches. A gap in the fog showed a storefront guarded by iron gates. Spaces. She stopped in front of a wide-windowed statue shop. Plaster-of-Paris figures. A bust of Lincoln. A fat-lipped, fat-stomached Buddha. Spaces. Round spaces. Little fat tummy. *Dumpling . . . little potbelly.* Spaces. The chalk-white figures seemed to leap at her. Gorillas, giraffes, unicorns, cats . . . little cat feet move on. . . . Moving on, her eyes moved from the animal figures to skinny-necked, belly-bloated vases, busts of famous composers, huge sailfish, starfish, nudes in every conceivable position. Legs, trunks, arms intertwined. Long spaces. Wriggled like worms.

Rosemary looked down at her feet. They had disappeared into a bank of fog. No feet. Spaces. Now, she passed a restaurant. Now, she passed under striped awnings. They hovered over her, their stripes undulating menacingly. She skated on and on and on.

A shooting gallery. Ducks. Stars. Shooting stars. In infinite space. She skated in space.

She peered into a tiny store window. A crystal ball, a plaster palm, a chart with signs of the Zodiac. "Mrs. Zena Whitewater, Fortuneteller." Spaces. "Mirror, mirror, on the wall, who's the fairest of them all?"

More spaces. Swirling, crashing black spaces.

Last shack on the pier. Bait. Tackle. Reserve space on a sportsfishing boat. License included. License for space.

At the end of the pier, Rosemary leaned over the rail and stared down into the inky water . . . tar? Spaces. And spaces and spaces and spaces as she watched the water boil, churn, and spew against the pilings of the pier. A towering blanket of fog moved slowly toward shore. She looked up at it. It came closer. It would soon cover her, wipe her out. She would be gone. Into the spaces. Drowned in spaces.

She would climb to the top of the fog bank. But it turned to water. Spaces of water. Her heart pounded painfully in her chest. What was on the other side of the fog? Spaces. On the other side of the fog was . . . space. Void, vacant space. Nothing.

Water was trickling down from the sheet of fog. The water was rushing, cascading. Now, it was torrential. The fog shaped itself into a monumental tidal wave. It hesitated at its crest, seemed to take a deep breath. Then it

GOODBYE, PAPER DOLL

crashed down . . . down . . . down. It engulfed her; she gasped for breath. No air. She thrashed around. Tried to breathe. She needed air . . . air . . . she needed space . . . space. . . .

She heard disjointed voices:

GIRL: Saw her about an hour ago.

GUY: Didn't say nuthin'. Spaced out.

GIRL: Musta O.D'd.

MAN: You said she had a car?

GUY: Parked over there.

SECOND MAN: Paramedics on the way.

WOMAN: Knew she was up to no good. Time I got to her, she was in a heap. On the pier. Like now.

MAN: Cover her. Might be in shock.

She heard the sound of sirens. Men's voices: "That's the way. Careful. Let'er go." More jumbled voices.

Then quiet. Beautiful, dreamless, serene. Tranquil spaces.

Nineteen

In and out of spaces. Dark, light, sound, silence.

Rosemary awakened to see a red neon sign: "Emergency Entrance." Lying on her back, she was wheeled down a corridor and into a brightly lit room. She shut her eyes against the glare.

She felt her eyelid being pulled up. "Let's get some blood," a male voice said.

She opened her eyes. A doctor was examining her fingernails. He bent to smell her breath.

A nurse swabbed her arm. "I'll need several tubes," the doctor said.

Rosemary felt the prick of a needle in her arm.

Her other arm was raised by the doctor. "No track marks," he said.

Now, an aid came into view. She held a notebook in which she was writing.

"Name?" said the doctor to the aid.

"Rosemary Norton."

"Rosemary?" the doctor said. "Rosemary, can you hear me?"

Rosemary turned her face from him, closed her eyes again. She just wanted to sleep. Why was he asking her name if he already knew it?

She opened her eyes to see dark, red blood rising in a syringe. She closed her eyes, opened them again. It was like looking through different windows. Now she saw a bottle of fluid being hung high above her head.

"Cut on the forehead. No stitches needed," the doctor said.

She let herself slip into a half sleep. She remembered a

childhood game she used to play with the other kids. They'd all join hands and hold them above their heads. Then they'd sing while the one who was "it" stepped in and out of the circle under their upraised hands. "Bluebird, bluebird, in and out my window/Bluebird, bluebird, in and out my window/Bluebird, bluebird, in and out my window/Oh, Johnnie, I am tired. . . ."

Someone was prodding at her stomach. Whoever was playing this game had it all wrong. They should be tapping on her shoulders. The kid who was "it" had to stop behind the child where the song paused, then begin tapping that child on the shoulders while the others sang a new refrain: "Take a little girl and tap her on the shoulders/Take a little girl and tap her on the shoulders/ Take a little girl and tap her on the shoulders/Oh, Johnnie, I am tired!"

She opened her eyes again. The doctor was speaking to a policeman: ". . . dehydration . . . fluids going . . . find out the name of the family doctor . . ."

Another ride. Ambulance? No sirens. Bottle of fluid still above her head. A young, white-coated man sitting beside her, his fingers on her pulse.

The sun was shining through the hospital room window. The shaft of light struck the intravenous bottle making each drop of fluid look like a multifaceted, rainbow-colored diamond.

Rosemary's mouth felt dry. She tried to swallow. Nothing. A nurse was standing beside her bed.

"Drink of water?" Rosemary said weakly.

"By all means," the nurse smiled. She helped Rosemary sip at the bent straw in the glass of tepid water. Then she straightened Rosemary's covers, checked the IV bottle, and went out.

Like a blind person reading a stranger's face, Rosemary let her thin fingers gently trace her own brow, slide over the bones beneath her eyebrows, follow the deep hollows in her cheeks, then touch the point of her chin. Her arm fell to her side, and she marveled at the long, long time it took for it to come to rest on the bed.

She was melting . . . floating . . . drifting. Transcended . . . above and independent of her body as if she were a vaporous cloud looking down upon it.

And yet she knew she was in control. Exhausted, but triumphant, she had overcome her body. She had overcome herself. *But had she? She still wasn't sure.*

Outside the door, the faint rise and fall of voices lullabied her into a light sleep.

Rosemary was starving herself to death. She was dying.

And she didn't know it.

When she awakened again, Rosemary saw Mom and Dad standing at her bedside.

"How do you feel, honey?" Mom asked. Her eyes were red, puffy.

"Okay. Fine."

"We've been out of our minds," Dad said.

"Sorry . . . I didn't mean to. . . ."

"Oh, Rosemary, darling . . . you'll never know . . . when the police called, we thought. . . ."

Dad put his hand on Mom's shoulder. "She's safe now," he said, tears welling in his eyes.

"I want to go home."

"Soon," Mom said. "When you're better."

"How long have I been here?"

"You don't remember seeing us during the night?" Mom asked.

Rosemary shook her head.

"You were brought in about one-thirty a.m. From that other hospital near the beach." Mom looked at her watch. "It's morning . . . ten-forty-five."

"Oh. Seems longer."

"Before you know it, you'll be home again," Dad said. He patted her hand, and let his tears fall unashamedly. "Please, sweetheart, just do what you're told."

"Okay," Rosemary said.

"We've got to go now," Mom said. "We'll see you this

Eighteen

Rosemary stopped the car at a traffic light. She basked in a warm glow. It felt so good to be warm and cozy in the car. Outside, a fine mist filmed the windshield. She flicked on the windshield wipers. A green arrow pointed her onto the freeway. The late-night traffic was light.

Driving in the righthand lane, she suddenly found herself making a right onto Sunset Boulevard. How had she gotten this far so quickly? Spaces lost, gone. The last thing she remembered was tying her shoelaces. No, there had been a green arrow somewhere since then. And lots of headlights shining in her eyes.

She turned up the heat. Ah, lovely. Like a hot summer's day. The windshield wipers sang a soothing song. Swish-whoosh, swish-whoosh, swish-whoosh, swish-whoosh. . . . It changed its words: *Skin-ee, skin-ee, skin-ee, skin-ee* . . . .

Rosemary listened with rapt pleasure: Swish-whoosh, *skin-ee, safe-tee, safe-tee, safe-tee, safe-tee.* . . .

She stopped at a dim red light. There seemed to be a thickened, milky halo around it. Fog? Spaces. Spaces of murky fog. Kenter Avenue. Kenter crossed Sunset Boulevard. Where had the freeway gone? Into some vast, timeless hole?

The shoulders of the curving road seemed to be hidden under shrublike billows of cloud. Rolls of sagebrush-fog divided to let the car pass, then clumped together again in shroudlike spaces.

The car followed the center divider of the road. Two yellow eyes approached. Headlights. The other car swerved out of her path and blasted its horn. She glanced in her rear-view mirror. The other car disappeared into a cave of fog. Swallowed up by foggy spaces. More clouds, remote spaces.

The dividing line in the road was no longer visible. Miscalculating the curves, she heard the sound of gravelly rocks falling off a cliff as the car bumped over a shoulder. She lurched it back onto the road.

The center dividing line reappeared, twisting around like an endless pain, like the end of a cartoon where the cat fades into the sunset. Cat. Fog. She kept the wheels on the center line. A line of broken spaces.

Cat. Fog. "The fog comes . . . cat feet . . ." she remembered from some poem. Cat feet move. Into spaces. The car moved into the right lane spiraling up and down, around and around. A lightning-shaped arrow directed the car past a canyon partly concealed by steam. Fog. Spaces. White plumes of spaces. Then the windshield wiper murmured comfortingly: *safe-tee,* swish-whoosh, *skin-ee, safe-tee.*

The car was warm and balmy and safe. It seemed to be held to the center of the road by an umbilical cord. *Safe-tee, Ma-ma, Ma-ma, safe-tee.* She was circled in the space of Mama's arms.

Charmed by the music of the windshield wipers, the road snaked up, up, coiling around and up again. A sudden, loud crunch of metal against rock and the car came to a dead stop. Rosemary's head hit the windshield, then snapped back. She turned off the ignition, put her fingers to her temple. A trickle of warm, sticky stuff oozed down her cheek. Was she hurt? There was no pain. There was only silence except for the clicking of the cooling engine and a faint spinning sound.

Though she could not see clearly, something told her to slide over to the right to get out of the car. The right front fender was crumpled into the side of a boulder. The left front wheel whirled crazily in the air over a deep ravine.

She carefully got back into the car and put it into reverse. The back wheels spun noisily, impotently. Then they grabbed, gained traction, and pulled the car free.

GOODBYE, PAPER DOLL

evening. We've got the best doctors, but . . . try, Rosemary . . . you've got to try!"

Rosemary didn't quite know what she was supposed to try to do. But she knew Mom and Dad were upset. She'd feel better if they went home, left her alone. An unexpected feeling of anger flooded through her. But she suppressed it, said what she thought would be expected of her: "I'll try. I'll be all right."

When her parents left the room, Rosemary looked around. She couldn't sit up. One arm was tied down, the needle and tube of the IV taped in place. She raised her head and neck as far as she could.

It was the usual sort of hospital room, pretending to be cheerful: busy print drapes at the window, a couple of pictures on the wall, a television set suspended from the ceiling. But despite the mint-green painted walls, the dark brown carpeted floor, and the loud-patterned drapes in brown and green, the room depressed her.

The door opened and Dr. Feinstein breezed in. He was followed by a tall middle-aged woman with gray hair.

As he walked to the foot of her bed, he smiled, "Hi, Rosemary. How're you feeling?"

Rosemary nodded glumly.

He turned to the attractive woman as he looked at Rosemary's chart. "Want to take a look? Fluids intravenously."

"I don't think so," the woman said. She looked at Rosemary. "I'd like an introduction though."

For some reason, Rosemary was glad the woman was not smiling, not putting on a happy face.

Dr. Feinstein came to Rosemary's side and gave her the usual kiss on the cheek. "Gave us quite a scare last night," he scolded. Then he smiled again. "Rosemary, meet Doctor Lillian Collens. Lillian, this beautiful child is Rosemary Norton."

The woman looked into Rosemary's eyes. "Hi, Rosemary," she said. "Feeling kind of bummed out, aren't you?"

Rosemary glared at her.

"Why don't I leave and let you two get to know each

other?" Dr. Feinstein suggested. "What do you say, Lillian?"

"Good idea," the woman said. She pulled up a chair, covered in the same loud-patterned fabric as the drapes. "Like your room?"

Rosemary shrugged. "Who designed it, Helen Keller?"

Dr. Collens laughed explosively. Rosemary was grudgingly pleased. Dr. Lillian Collens was human. Rosemary had to give her that.

"Okay," Dr. Collens said. "Let's get down to business. You're here to get well. I'm here to help you do that. We're going to have to do a lot of talking—both of us—to get at the root of your problem. You want to talk first?"

"I don't feel like talking," Rosemary said sullenly.

"Fine," said Dr. Collens. "I like to talk." She reached over and rang the nurse's call bell attached to the pillow. "I also like coffee. It's one of my several vices."

She leaned back into the chair and kicked off her shoes. Rosemary looked at her. Something about the doctor reminded Rosemary of the Countess. Of course, she was much younger. And she was dressed much more smartly. She looked as if she were ready to model the latest fashions for the mature woman. But still, she was ... what was it?

And then Rosemary knew what it was. The doctor was *comfortable*. She was honest, open, and comfortable. But Rosemary would not change her stance of anger. She would not let this comfortable woman get the best of her.

A nurse poked her head into the room. "Something you need, doctor?"

"Lots of coffee," Dr. Collens said.

The nurse laughed. "I put on a fresh pot as soon as I saw the whites of your eyes. I'll bring it right in."

"Thanks, Rae Ann," laughed the doctor. She turned to Rosemary. "Where were we? Oh, yes, I talk, you listen, right?"

Rosemary tightened her lips, but the doctor didn't seem to notice.

"All right," said Dr. Collens. "First I'll tell you a little

GOODBYE, PAPER DOLL

about me. I'm a psychiatrist. That means I'm concerned with both your medical and emotional health. Together with Doctor Feinstein, we'll get your physical problems under control. But you and I, we'll have to work together to ferret out why you want to do this to yourself."

Rosemary smirked. Together, she thought. What does she think I am, some kind of infant? Anything she finds out, she'll have to discover by herself.

The nurse brought a carafe of coffee and cups.

"Thanks, Rae Ann," the doctor said to the nurse's retreating back. "You're a doll."

"Anytime," Rae Ann laughed as she left the room.

Dr. Collens poured coffee for herself and put a fresh cup within Rosemary's reach.

"Now, about anorexia nervosa . . . the disease. I want you to know up-front, that the real illness is not about dieting, not about being skinny or fat. The weight business is only a symptom. The real question is how you feel about you."

She paused and waited for Rosemary to respond. In the silence that followed Rosemary thought angrily: I'd feel fine about myself if everybody would just leave me alone. What do they want from me? I get top grades at school; I work; I keep myself trim. But even that's not good enough for *me*. I have to be better, best.

As if she had all the time in the world, the doctor sipped at her coffee.

"Let me tell you about some other girls . . . women . . . with your problem. It doesn't matter what other people think of them. Their trouble is that no matter what others think, and no matter what they achieve, it's never good enough. Never good enough for *them*. Their major fear is that they're not living up to expectations . . . other people's and their own. They often fear that they just might be the same as the next guy . . . average, ordinary."

Trying to keep a straight face, Rosemary felt a sudden shock. How did this woman know her innermost secrets? Had she had the same illness herself? Maybe she had. She certainly was angular enough. Or, thought Rosemary, did she have some kind of gift for mind reading?

As if in answer to Rosemary's unspoken questions, Dr. Collens continued: "I've had many anorexic patients. Each one—without exception—came to me thinking she was something quite special, unique."

Rosemary's attempt to be remote, distant, broke down. She felt a stir of fear. Fear and desolation. All this time, she had felt she was, indeed, different, extraordinary. Now she was finding out that there were lots of girls who were identical to her. That was far from flattering. She felt deflated, depressed. Feeling her tears surface, she turned away from the doctor.

But there was no stopping Dr. Lillian Collens. She kept on talking away. Psychiatrists keep quiet, make the *patient* talk, Rosemary thought dourly. Lies!

"There's nothing supernatural about your sickness, Rosemary. I hate to disappoint you, but what you're suffering from is unfortunately common. Obsessive dieting begins with fear, anxiety. What you're getting out of it is proof to yourself that you can do what others can't. It's a way of showing yourself you have control."

Control, thought Rosemary bitterly. I can't even control these idiotic tears. But she wouldn't let the doctor know what she was feeling. She kept her face turned away, refused to utter a word.

She heard the doctor stand up. "Think about what I've said." The doctor sounded matter-of-fact, sure of herself. "I'll be in to see you tomorrow."

Rosemary felt the doctor's hand on her shoulder. Her voice became more gentle. "It's okay to be human," the doctor said. "I've never met anyone who was otherwise."

After Rosemary heard the door close, she stared at the ceiling. She could feel the tears run down into her ears. Some of the things the doctor had said struck a chord deep inside her. Was there something to be learned . . . something to be gained by considering her words?

"No, no, no!" Rosemary said aloud. She hadn't come this far just to be undone by some weirdo psychiatrist! She wasn't as weak-minded as that doctor thought!

Rosemary was ready to do battle with Dr. Lillian Collens, a battle unto death.

Twenty

Her mother was at the hospital before dinnertime. "We talked to Doctor Collens," she said. "Hope you like her as much as we do."

Rosemary grunted, sulking.

"We'll be seeing her as a family. On a regular basis. Seems we can all use some help."

"I don't need any help," Rosemary blurted out. "You want to see that creep, go ahead. I'll get out of here on my own."

"You're sick, Rosemary. You have to——"

Rosemary interrupted. "There's nothing wrong with me!"

"You've got to cooperate, honey . . . please. . . ." Her mother was crying.

"I want out!" Rosemary shouted.

"You can't . . . not yet . . . the doctor said . . ."

"Bull!" Rosemary screamed. "That shrink's handing you a bunch of crap and you're buying it!"

"Try to understand, Rosemary. We have to follow doctor's orders to help you get well. We love you . . . we'll do anything . . . please, darling. . . ."

Mama, Mama, don't abandon me . . . don't leave me alone, Rosemary thought. *I'm afraid . . . I'm so scared!*

"Mama . . . Mama . . ." she whimpered.

"We'll come often . . . your friends can visit. Please, be good . . . eat. . . ." Mom said tearfully.

"Take me home," Rosemary pleaded.

"As soon as I can, honey. The minute we're permitted."

By dinnertime, Rosemary had worked her fear up to a full-blown resentment. Her parents didn't care what happened to her. They didn't give a damn. They'd let her rot in this lousy place till she died. And if she did die, it would be their fault. They'd all be responsible, Dr. Feinstein, Dr. Collens, and good old Mom and Dad.

A young nurse, carrying a tray, came into the room. "Hi," she said, rolling up the table and setting the tray down. "My name's Chris, what's yours?" The nurse looked like a teenager.

"Rosemary."

"I've got good news for you, Rosemary," Chris said brightly. "Orders to discontinue the IV . . . see how you do on your own."

Chris gently removed the needle and rolled the IV stand away. She helped Rosemary sit up, then pushed the tray closer. "Mmm, smells good," said Chris as she lifted the metal cover off the plate. "Do me a favor and clean it all up." She started out of the room "Hate to have to put the IV back later. Check you soon."

Rosemary stared down at the food. Salad, chicken, mashed potatoes, string beans. And that was only the beginning. There was also bread and butter, milk, and tapioca pudding. She had been told she could order anything she wanted, her favorite foods. So she had checked items on the menu that she thought would look impressive to the doctors.

But she was in a quandry. If she didn't eat it, it would be reported and they'd stick her with that damned IV and force calories into her. If she did eat it, that shrink would get the satisfaction she wanted. Either way, she'd get fat. No way out of that one.

Another, more important matter: suppose she felt like bingeing? What if she began craving food and there was nothing to eat?

When the compulsion to binge came upon her, it was something physical, animal, beyond control. There was no way to ward off the demon of hunger except to binge. But

GOODBYE, PAPER DOLL

she comforted herself with the knowledge that bingeing was safe; she could always throw up afterward.

Her stomach knotted with anxiety. She couldn't think. She needed time to sort out the alternatives. There had to be an answer. Then she sighed with relief.

She could beat it. All she had to do was hide some food in case she wanted it later. Her plate would be emptied, one point for me, she thought. No more calorie-filled IV, two points for me. Backup food for a good, satisfying binge during the night, three points for me! I win . . . they lose!

Chris came in to take the tray and flashed a delighted smile. "Terrific!" she said. "Ya' done good! I'll switch the television on for you."

When the door swung shut, Rosemary reached for the controls and switched the set off. She relaxed and leaned back into her pillows. She had pulled it off. What a jerk Chris was! Simple-minded! A pushover! Rosemary smiled. Four points for me, she thought smugly.

Rosemary was staring disinterestedly at an inane game show on the television set when the door opened. It was Trudy carrying a vase of flowers. She stopped just inside the door. "Can I come in?"

Rosemary sat up and looked at her. One hand still on the door, Trudy looked as if she didn't know whether she'd be welcome or not.

"Come on in, nerd," Rosemary said.

Grinning, Trudy came farther into the room and set the flowers down on the bedside table. Then her smile froze. "God, Rosemary, you look awful!"

"Thanks."

"I didn't mean . . . I just . . . your mother said you were sick, but I didn't know. . . ." Trudy fumbled.

"I'll live," said Rosemary with a lot more bravado than she felt.

Embarrassed, Trudy looked down at her shoes. When she met Rosemary's eyes again, her own were filled with tears.

Rosemary blinked. Why did she always want to cry when she saw someone else's tears?

"Oh, Rosemary!" cried Trudy, sitting on the bed. She started to say something but her tears stopped her. She shook her head, then without warning, she took Rosemary into her arms.

And together, the girls wept into each other's shoulders. "You'll be my best friend forever . . . like a sister," Trudy cried.

When they parted, Rosemary looked at Trudy's tear-streaked face. "I . . . didn't . . . think you cared," Rosemary stammered.

The two stared at one another. Rosemary giggled. Trudy began to chuckle. Without quite knowing that they were relieving their own tension, they broke into laughter. And the laughter grew and built into screaming hilarity. Chris rushed in to see what the ruckus was all about.

"I didn't think you cared!" Rosemary said to Chris.

At Chris's astonished expression, they howled even louder.

Coming closer, Chris began to smile, then she grinned, and by the time she reached the bed, all three of them were convulsed in crazy, contagious laughter.

Her sister Amy's face flashed through Rosemary's mind, and as she laughed, she knew she'd be calling Amy to apologize for the abominable way she had treated her the last time they met.

Rosemary slept through the night without having to binge, and breakfast was easy. The moment she was left alone with her tray, she limped painfully to the bathroom and flushed the food down the toilet.

Back in bed, she tried to find a comfortable position, but it was impossible. If she lay on her side, she ached from her shoulders to her knees. If she lay on her back, there was a red-hot tingling pain from her neck to her rear. It was as if the bed were made of cement. She sat up and tucked one of her pillows under her knees.

That's how Dr. Feinstein saw her when he came in. Even before greeting her, he checked the chart.

"When can I get out of here?" Rosemary challenged.

Dr. Feinstein shook his head. "Whenever you decide."

"I've decided. I want to leave now."

"Nothing doing," said the doctor. "Not until there's some improvement. You're not even maintaining. Your weight has *dropped* half a pound since you've been admitted."

Rosemary said nothing while he peered at her chart.

"If I gain weight I can go?"

"Yep," said Dr. Feinstein. "But you've got to be eating on your own." He came to stand beside her. "We can't chance it, otherwise."

"How much? How much would I have to gain?"

The doctor looked at her closely. "A few pounds—five, maybe a little more. It would take no time at all . . . if you really wanted to do it."

Rosemary felt cornered, trapped. The room seemed to close in on her. The very idea of gaining all that weight was harrowing. She wanted to run, fly. She had to escape!

The doctor took her hand. "Listen to me, darling. I know you want to feel good. I know you want to feel happy and healthy. But what you don't know is that you've begun to get your kicks out of feeling rotten. What does that prove?"

What does he know? thought Rosemary resentfully. Even if she could explain it, he wouldn't understand what it was like to be exquisitely fragile. How could he know the dazzling feeling that resulted from fasting? Testing, stretching to the limit gave her an heroic, exalted perception of herself that verged on the religious.

Walking a tightrope, pushing herself to the extreme was a rarefied, glorious phenomenon. Resolving to be the master of her body, she refused to succumb to his utter insensitivity.

Getting no response from Rosemary, the doctor went on: "For a minute, think of your body as a machine, a beautiful car, a Rolls-Royce. You've told me how much you love your own car. Would you let it rust, run down? Would you neglect it? Your body can give you fine performance. Like a car, it can give you distance . . . a certain mileage. But only if you take good care of it, only if you give it fuel."

Rosemary wished the doctor would stop droning on and on, stop lecturing. She forced herself to yawn rudely in his face.

He flushed and Rosemary knew she'd gotten a rise out of him. Good, she thought. If he wanted to take her on, she was ready for him. Like a gladiator girded for an awesome confrontation, she knew she could defeat him.

Dr. Feinstein sighed heavily. "I don't want to frighten you, but I think the time has come to talk about it. If you don't begin to get better, and soon, there will be more intravenous, or tube feeding. And if that doesn't help, we'll have to start hyperalimentation."

"What's that?" Rosemary said warily.

"Surgery."

"Surgery! For not eating? What would you take out?"

"Not to take out," the doctor said. "To put in . . . nutrition . . . to keep you alive."

"I don't believe you!" said Rosemary, outraged.

"Believe me. A tube will be inserted in your chest below the collarbone. You'll have nothing by mouth for a while. But you will have your nutritional needs met."

"You're lying . . . using scare tactics!" Rosemary yelled.

"We'd rather not force-feed you. But if there's no other way, the tube will be taped to your shoulder and a bottle, with nutrition in it, will be on a stand. You can walk around with it. Wherever you go, it goes. That what you want?" the doctor said firmly.

Rosemary clenched her jaws tightly, the muscles in her cheek twitching. She was scared almost senseless.

As if he had said nothing radical, Dr. Feinstein bent down and kissed her as usual. Then he turned and left the room.

But as frightened as she was of the surgery, Rosemary was even more terrified of getting fat. When her lunch arrived, she pushed the tray aside.

Twenty-one

Chris shook the thermometer down and put it into Rosemary's mouth. She noted the pulse rate on the chart. "See you refused lunch today. Food that bad?"

Rosemary nodded. Chris removed the thermometer, read it, and wrote on the chart. "It does get kinda yecchy at times," she said. "Want some ice cream?"

"No, thanks," Rosemary said.

Chris looked at her. "Listen, when I go on my break, I can pick something up for you—hamburger, cake, pie, pizza. You're on a totally unrestricted diet. What would you like?"

"Nothing," Rosemary said. "Thanks, anyway."

"Better have something. IV's scheduled if you don't eat voluntarily by the end of the day."

"Maybe later."

"Look, Rosemary, I've seen kids like you. It's a losing battle. May as well eat and get out of here. If you don't, they'll——"

"I don't want to hear about it!"

"Okay, okay," said Chris. "Don't say I didn't warn you."

She switched the television set on. "If you change your mind, give me a ring."

Chris and Dr. Collens exchanged greetings at the door. "I'll bring the coffee," Chris said to the doctor as she left.

Dr. Collens checked the chart and came to sit beside Rosemary. She kicked off her shoes and put her eyeglasses up over her hair. She looked at Rosemary.

"I don't have to ask how you are," she said.

"I'm fine," Rosemary said sullenly. "When do I get out?"

"You know the answer to that one," said Dr. Collens. "Eat three meals, snacks in between. Couple of weeks, maybe. Then we'll see."

Chris brought the carafe and cups and went back out.

Dr. Collens filled both cups, put sugar and cream in Rosemary's, and pushed it toward her. Then she sipped her coffee. "Feel like talking today?"

"No!" Rosemary shot back, spoiling for a fight.

The doctor leaned into her chair. "I will then," she said. "Feeling superior is all right. Accomplishment is okay. Discipline, control, are fine. Dieting, in and of itself, is okay. All of these things can be constructive . . . if they are not done excessively. If doing these things could solve your basic problem, I'd say go ahead and do them. The problem is that you're not in touch with what your problems *are*."

Riddles, thought Rosemary. Circular conversation. The doctor was trying to confuse her, make her feel like some stupid kid.

"What you really want might be very simple," said Dr. Collens. "You're just going about it in a terribly complicated manner." She poured more coffee while Rosemary thought about what she said.

Simple! Nothing is simple, Rosemary thought. Give your all, your best, and what do you get? Harassment, punishment, persecution.

"Most, if not all, anorexics want basically the same things as other teenagers. They want to grow and mature, be responsible, independent people."

The words sounded saccharine to Rosemary. What she *didn't* want was anybody preaching at her, patronizing her, treating her like an imbecile!

"Are you finished?" said Rosemary archly. "I'm tired."

Dr. Collens looked at her over the rim of her coffee cup. Unruffled, she set the cup down. "It used to make you feel great to please other people, do what they expected of you and more. That didn't cut it. Now it makes you feel good to do what nobody else can do. But that doesn't solve your problems, either."

Rosemary was beginning to feel a certain uneasiness. The doctor was getting too close, incisive.

Dr. Collens leaned forward. Her voice took on a more conversational tone. "Rosemary, a basic problem of most anorexics is that they don't know how to *constructively do exactly what they want to do* . . . probably don't *know* exactly what they want to do. They feel forced to take extreme measures to *prove to themselves that they're worthwhile human beings.*"

Rosemary turned her face away. She liked the doctor better when she sounded tough. When she softened, it melted her own defenses. There was nothing to strike at, fight with.

"You *have* the right to live your own life, do what you want to do and not suffer guilt for it. You don't need to apologize, defend, or be guilty about it." The doctor paused. "Look at me, Rosemary."

Rosemary felt suddenly drawn to the doctor's words. She looked into her eyes.

"It's not easy to become your own person. You've tried to do it first by living up to what you think your family expects of you, your own unrealistic expectations. Now, you've tried to do it by losing all that weight. You've denied yourself food, enjoyment, fun, friends.

"Rosemary, dear, all your preoccupation with food, the diet, your illness is your way of *not* dealing with the deeper problems. You're not accomplishing anything by avoiding the other dilemmas.

"There's usually not one 'key' problem . . . one 'real' problem that causes anorexia nervosa. Most times, it's more complicated than that." The doctor sighed. "We honestly don't know all we'd like to about the syndrome."

Rosemary wanted to lash biting words back at the doctor. She wanted to shock her with scathing sarcasm, but she could do nothing but stare at her. It was as if Rosemary were the wicked witch of Oz, and she was melting into nothingness.

"I know you think you've already been doing the ultimate in sacrificing. But to get well, there's more to come. You'll have to sacrifice pride in inappropriate actions and attitudes, feeling superspecial.

"You'll have to learn to express your likes and dislikes, even if it displeases someone else. And that will involve therapy with your whole family as well as my seeing you one-to-one.

"It won't be easy, and it may take a long time, but in the end, you truly *can* be in control."

Her eyes still riveted on the doctor's face, Rosemary watched her finish off her coffee and lean back.

"Maybe you'll find out that you're not above the crowd, after all. But you won't be all alone anymore."

Disconsolately, Rosemary stared at the television set in the semidark room. Soap opera. The leading lady was attempting to poison the leading man. She had dropped some poison into his mint julep.

What rot, thought Rosemary. But she tucked the pillow under her knees and tried to make herself comfortable in spite of the sharp pain at the bony base of her spine.

The leading lady was urging the man to drink his mint julep. They went around and around about it, killing time, if not the man. Then, just as he put the glass to his lips, the music swelled and the announcer said: "Tune in tomorrow for the next exciting episode of...."

"Rosie?"

Rosemary snapped her head around to see Jason standing at her bedside.

"You *were* sick," he said. "I knew it."

Rosemary drew the blanket up to her chin. "What're you doing here?"

"Didn't know your brain was affected. I'm visiting you, what do you think? The Countess wanted to come too, but she had a cold and thought she'd better wait until later."

Rosemary looked up at him. She could barely make out his features with the window shade drawn. Her pleasure at seeing him was tinged with anxiety. What would he demand of her?

GOODBYE, PAPER DOLL

"Looks like the black hole of Calcutta in here," said Jason as he went to the window and drew up the shade. Coming back to the bed, he sat down on it and took her hand and kissed it. "God, Rosie, I've been so lonely for you."

Rosemary swallowed a lump in her throat. His touch felt good.

Now, Jason looked into her eyes. "Rosie, you gotta get well. You just gotta. I need you." He took her into his arms and rocked her. "Little Rosie, darling. . . ." He kissed her forehead, her eyes, her cheeks. "I want you so much. Come back to me." He kissed her on the lips, held her closer.

Rosemary passively let him kiss her. "Jason, Jason, I'm so scared."

Jason buried his face in her neck. "Sweet Rosie, Rosie." He took her by the shoulders, held her at arm's length. "Let me look at you, get to know you again."

The two smiled into each other's eyes.

"Aha! Gotcha!" laughed Chris as she came into the room carrying a glass of apple juice.

Jason released Rosemary and sat down on the chair. Chris put the glass on the bedside table. "Don't let me interrupt you. Just go on with what you were doing," she teased. "Haven't been involved in a juicy, erotic scene since last night on television."

"Sorry, but you're not involved in this one, either," Jason said. "I'm a one-woman man."

"My loss," Chris joked. "I'll just leave you two lovebirds alone." She paused at the door. "But remember, this is a hospital, not a drive-in. No serious fooling around!"

Jason laughed as she exited. "She's okay," he said.

"Yeah, the only human one around here."

"Since you've asked, I'll tell you what's new," Jason said. "In order of importance. My dad's coming home in fifteen days, three hours, and twenty minutes. Did all my Christmas shopping for him already. Don't want to waste a minute while he's here."

"How long will he stay?"

"Through New Year's. Boy, this'll be a Christmas I'll never forget!"

"Jason, I'm so glad."

His eyes shone as he spoke. "I'm getting everything I wanted for Christmas! Dad. You. All of us together."

Rosemary smiled at his happiness. Reluctant to spoil it, she didn't tell him she had no idea how long she'd be in the hospital.

"Next item," Jason said. "I was going to save this to surprise you, but I think you can use a little cheer-up. Know that picture of you? The one with your face all smudged?"

"What about it?"

"I entered it in the photo contest at school. It's been judged one of the best three. They'll be pinned up in the main corridor and the kids get to vote for the best one."

Rosemary stiffened. "You promised me you wouldn't show any of my pictures."

"But this is different. You're gorgeous in that picture. It'll get first award. I'm sure."

"I don't want my picture pinned up at school!"

"Come on, Rosie, it's an honor."

"For you or for me?" Rosemary sniped.

"What're you talking about?"

"About you!" She couldn't control her rage. "You don't care anything about *me* . . . never did. . . ."

"I love you. You know that."

"I know you love my pictures . . . my image . . . not really me!"

Jason tried for lightness. "I'm doomed. I love your pictures, your image, your temper—the works."

"No, you don't!" yelled Rosemary. "You don't even know who I am! You don't want to know!"

"You got it all wrong, Rosie, listen———"

"You're the one who's got it wrong! All you love is what you see! Nothing else! You just want to use me! My body . . . the way I look. . . ."

Jason stood up clenching his fists, his face white with anger. His voice shook with emotion. "You're so stupidly wrapped up in yourself, you don't know anything about love!"

He grasped a corner of her blanket and whipped it down to her ankles. Rosemary's hospital gown was tangled midway up her thighs. Her legs were drawn up, the pillow tucked under her knees.

Rosemary tried to sit up, reach for the blanket, but he pushed her back down. He took a long look at her from her toes to her face. Her bony knees were exposed, her sharp elbows stuck out of her sleeves.

"Look at yourself!" he said. "Like a grasshopper . . . an insect! Who could love you for your body? I'm the one who's gotta be crazy, all right! You're ugly . . . ugly! Starving yourself to death! But, God help me, I still love you!"

Now Rosemary pulled the blanket back up under her chin. "Get out! Get out of here and don't come back!"

That night the IV was reinserted into Rosemary's arm.

Twenty-two

The next day, Chris came into the room to check the IV. "It's dark as a cave in here. I'll raise the shade."

"No," Rosemary said.

"Come on, Rosemary, let a little sunshine in."

"No."

Chris sniffed. "Some fresh air wouldn't hurt, either." She started for the window.

"Leave it shut."

Chris came back to the bed. "So you had a little tiff with your guy. It'll blow over. He'll be back."

Staring straight ahead, Rosemary kept silent.

"Not worth killing yourself."

No answer from Rosemary.

Chris bent down and stroked Rosemary's forehead. "Believe me, honey, I've been through these things myself. It'll be——" She stopped and sniffed the air. "What's that awful smell?"

Disinterestedly, Rosemary watched Chris open the drawer of the bedside table. "Oh, geeze," said Chris, bringing out a dish of spoiled tapioca pudding. "Phew!" She set the dish on the table. "What else did you stash away?" She rummaged in the drawer and came up with a carton of soured milk. Setting it aside, she looked soberly at Rosemary. "I'm sorry, but I'll have to report this. Hoarding food's a vital symptom."

Another betrayal, thought Rosemary. She should have expected it. Well, what difference did it make? Who cared? It didn't matter. Nothing mattered.

"I really am sorry," said Chris, putting her hand on Rosemary's shoulder.

GOODBYE, PAPER DOLL 143

Without looking at her, Rosemary shrugged Chris's hand off.

Chris sighed. She picked up the stinking food and, holding it away from her, went out of the room.

She'd have to be more careful next time, thought Rosemary. Find a better hiding place. Or binge on the stuff before it spoiled. Eat, throw up . . . eat, throw up . . . eat . . . eat . . . eat . . . .

Her stomach cramped with hunger. She was ravenous. She pictured chocolate cake, moist, thickly frosted, double layered. She thought of a heap of mashed potatoes dripping with rich gravy. Food . . . food . . . food . . . all kinds, all textures, colors. Like spinning pinwheels, ice-cream sundaes, candy bars, pizzas, roast turkeys, candied sweet potatoes, creamed asparagus, rich puddings circled in her mind.

She had to stop it . . . stop it . . . calories . . . fat . . . gross . . . obese. . . .

She looked up at the IV bottle spilling its hated contents into her. She had to stop it . . . *stop it!*

She reached over with her other hand and pulled the needle out of her arm. The strike of pain was like an exclamation point at the end of a sentence. Sentence. Jail sentence. How long would she be penalized, punished? Jail sentence. Death sentence? Who cared? What difference did it make? She shuddered. Death sentence?

She'd think of something else. What? Skating at the beach. Fish and chips, candy apples, hotdogs. No, not food. Something else. Driving over the canyon. Walnut trees. Orange trees. Nuts . . . oranges . . . bananas . . . pineapple. Her mouth watered at the thought of tart fruit. Stop thinking about food! Think about swimming. Poolside. The umbrella table loaded with lemonade . . . barbequed ribs . . . pickles . . . macaroni salad . . . olives . . . hot garlic bread . . . watermelon. . . .

Stop it! Stop thinking about food! Stop it! Stop it! Stop it!

She switched on the television set. She'd get her mind off food. She'd concentrate on the TV.

The leading man had the mint julep at his lips when the telephone at his side rang. He put down the drink.

The camera focused on the leading lady. "Let it ring," she said. "Drink up, drink up."

A shot of the man's hand reaching for the telephone. His voice: "Hello, oh hi, sweetie. . . ."

The woman's face. She looked as if she were in mortal agony.

The man, holding his mint julep close to his mouth. He put the glass to his lips. He looked stunned, put the glass back down.

The television picture went to black. Then a newscaster's face: "We interrupt this program for a special news bulletin! Jason Galanter, world-famed photojournalist, covering the uprising in the Middle East, has been fatally shot. No other details have been released."

Rosemary sat straight up.

"I repeat," said the newscaster, "the prominent American newsman, Jason Galanter, was killed early this morning by a demonstrator's stray bullet. We'll keep you updated as more information comes in. And now, back to your regularly scheduled program."

Rosemary sat frozen. She could feel goose bumps up and down her arms. *Jason's father! Oh, my God!*

Rosemary pushed her call button. "Chris! Chris! Please, Chris, come . . . hurry!"

Chris ran into the room to find Rosemary hysterical, rocked by the horrible news. Choking with sobs, Rosemary pointed to the TV set, where the newscaster was now repeating the message over scenes of a man, mortally wounded, falling under the feet of a churning mob. "Jason's father!" she cried. "I've got to get to Jason . . . I've got to go . . . I've got to see Jason!"

Flicking off the set, Chris tried to take her into her arms, but with all her strength, she pushed Chris off and staggered to the closet. Yanking her clothes from their hangers, she kept up a steady chant: ". . . got to get to Jason . . . must see Jason . . . I've got to go . . . got to go . . ." Then her knees buckled and she was about to sink to the floor when she felt Chris's arms around her waist. Dazed, numb, she let Chris lead her back to her bed. Murmuring soft words, Chris helped her lie down. Then she re-inserted the IV and told her that she'd call Dr. Collens at once.

Alone in her room, her energy spent, Rosemary could think only of one thing. She had to get out of the hospital. She had to get to Jason. But how? The only way out was for her to gain weight. And the only way to do that was to eat. She stiffened in panic. Eat? Impossible! There *was* no way out.

Later, at her bedside, Dr. Collens was sympathetic but brisk. "Before you can help Jason, you have to be willing to help yourself," she said, after she had heard Rosemary's pleas, arguments, demands to be discharged from the hospital. "You haven't gained an ounce since you've been here. You're barely maintaining."

Something inside Rosemary exploded. It was as if a new person had taken over the old one inside her. "You're a fool!" she screamed. "Who are you to tell me to help myself! I'm an expert at it! Nobody else gives a damn!"

She noted a sparkle in Dr. Collen's eyes as the doctor backed away and sat down in a chair. She was at least getting a rise out of her. "I'm alone . . . always have been . . . I do things for myself, by myself!"

The doctor was sitting straight up, leaning forward. "How about your family . . . friends?"

At this point the old Rosemary would have clammed up. But the new character . . . the strange, enraged Rosemary refused to be stilled. "Family!" she shrieked. "Who, Daddy? Cheat . . . liar . . . he doesn't know me, doesn't want to! Wants little Miss America . . . to make him look good! Mom? Sure, so long as I fit into her decor she's happy! Anything off-center and she'd topple! And sweet sister Amy? She's one of *them* . . . keeps it that way, wants it that way! She's in, I'm out!"

The new Rosemary's voice rose. And even the tone, shrill, piercing, sounded like a stranger's. "I'm always on the outs! At school . . . the girls . . . keeping me out of their snobby circle! Boys . . . look through me, not at me!

"I hate them . . . all of them! I don't need them . . . don't want them . . . don't need their help . . . yours either! I don't care . . . I don't care . . ." And then her voice broke.

The doctor stared at her while the new Rosemary faded and the old one surfaced. Rosemary turned her head and began to cry softly. "I do care . . . I do. I want to be on the inside." Dr. Collens thrust a tissue into Rosemary's hand, but still said nothing.

How dumb could I get? Rosemary thought, hating herself. My only way out of this dungeon is through this woman, and after that idiotic outburst, I'll never get out. I blew it . . . but good!

"I've been waiting for this," the doctor said quietly. "It's about time. I'm proud of you."

Rosemary looked at her. "For the first time, I hear you telling me what you want . . . what you need," The doctor said soberly.

Rosemary's eyes widened unbelievingly. The doctor was condoning a temper tantrum? She wasn't mad at her?

"We all feel the need to belong," Dr. Collens went on. "But sometimes, if we think we're on the outs anyway, it's easier to reject people *before* they do it to us. We send out messages that say, 'keep out.'"

"You mean it's all my fault?" Rosemary said edgily.

"Not at all. I mean I can't blame you for wanting to make yourself feel better . . . safer. It's scary to feel all alone. A lot of kids—anorexics particularly—tell themselves that they're afraid of getting too fat because it's somehow easier to be afraid of that than of what really scares them."

"But that's crazy!" Rosemary felt stricken. "Am *I* crazy?"

"What does crazy mean to you?"

"Crazy! Out of my mind! Out of this world!"

Dr. Collens reached out and took her hand. She smiled reassuringly. "All it means—in your case—is that your feelings are mixed up. Your head is giving you incorrect

GOODBYE, PAPER DOLL

signals . . . false fears. When we separate the fake fears from the real ones, we have a good chance of stopping them."

Tears spilling down her face, her voice almost a whisper, Rosemary said, "I don't understand. How can we tell which are which?"

"You've already made a good beginning by sharing your feelings. But you'll have to do a lot more of that. It won't be fun . . . It'll be hard, but it will work."

Rosemary kept her eyes down, feeling confused and miserable. She thought the doctor would hate her for screaming at her, and now she was all but being congratulated. She tried to sort out her thoughts. All she knew for certain was that she wanted to see Jason. The doctor was proud of her for telling what she needed . . . wanted. Okay, then. She'd get around her that way. "I need to see Jason. I want to get out, to go to him."

Shaking her head, Dr. Collens sighed and leaned back in her chair. "You didn't get sick overnight, you won't be all well tomorrow. Even after you're discharged, there'll be long-term therapy."

Rosemary glared at the doctor.

"But I promise you," said Dr. Collens, "you'll never be on the outs with me. No matter what."

Twenty-three

Rosemary repeatedly telephoned Jason. He wouldn't come to the phone. She wrote several notes to him. He didn't answer them. When she talked to the Countess, she was told that Jason wouldn't speak, wouldn't come out of his room, wouldn't allow his grandmother to come in.

And as the long hospital days dragged by, Rosemary swung from earnest cooperation with Dr. Collens, to open rebellion against her. Still, she began to share her deepest feelings, more and more each day. Sometimes she talked about her temptations to binge. Other times she talked about her sexual fears. She talked about her weight, her feelings about her body, her lack of self-worth. She bragged, raved about herself; she flagellated, denigrated herself.

At times the discussions were calm and pleasant, at other times violent. Rosemary disclosed raw, ugly feelings that had been festering for years. And despite her fear of exposure, she kept on talking. She had to test the doctor. Testing, she tried to trip her up, shake her promise to stick with her. Testing, she said things for deliberate shock effect. Testing, she raged and screamed. She binged and she fasted. She sulked, refusing to utter a word, then went on empty, meaningless, talking jags. But Dr. Collens steadfastly listened and commented, argued and discussed. She questioned and probed. She stuck with Rosemary throughout.

And then there were the harrowing days of the family group therapy meetings in the dayroom of the hospital. Even Amy came home from school to attend. The old, frightened Rosemary smiled, praised, pleased the others.

The new, rebellious Rosemary swore, accused, and shocked them. She evoked tears and recriminations, quarrels and name-calling. Dad was defensive and aggressive in turns; Mom, at once apologetic and complaining. Amy played the role of protective sister, then the intellectual mediator, and then the competitive sibling.

Dr. Collens, as facilitator, pointed out established family patterns, encouraged free expression of feelings, but kept a low profile, allowing the family to try different, more constructive ways of dealing with one another. But always Rosemary felt her encouraging presence. Despite her resistance to change, her embarrassment at exposure, her fear of displeasure from the family, Rosemary began to realize she could count on Dr. Collens. The doctor would not lie to her, nor let her down; she would stick to her no matter what. Rosemary trusted her.

And what eventually emerged was a blending of the old Rosemary and the new. She slowly gathered courage to tell her family exactly how she felt at being shut out. Painfully, she began to understand her family's weaknesses, hopes, fears. Gradually, she came to know Amy's defenses as the "plain one" in the family. She began to see her mother's need for orderliness and her father's fear of failure. But it was only when she became aware of her own struggles to fit into the family that she realized they all loved her—each in their own ways—and she could accept that love.

Rosemary was listening rather than watching a TV show. She turned it off when Trudy came in, armed with a live fish in a bowl. She set it down with a packet of fish food on the bedside table. "Got you something to play with."

"Thanks," said Rosemary. "It's darling."

Trudy looked down at Rosemary, then quickly turned away. "Yeah," she said. "Don't forget to feed it."

"You don't have to be sarcastic."

"Sorry," Trudy said.

"I *am* making progress, you know."

"Sure."

"I am! Even Dr. Collens says so. Learning new things about myself every day."

"Such as?"

"Such as learning to express my feelings *honestly* . . . anger, fear . . . love."

Trudy stared down at her. Rosemary could tell she was struggling to keep her mouth shut.

"You picking a fight?" Rosemary asked.

"No."

"Then what?"

"I'd better not say it."

"Say it."

"I just can't understand it, that's all. All the crap about *your* feelings. How about *my* feelings? Think it's fun to see you this way?"

"You can leave anytime you please."

"Not yet. You asked me to say it so I will. You've been going over the same ground for weeks. Aren't you bored, taking your emotional temperature every ten minutes?"

"I can't help it. I'm sick. I'm . . . I'm. . . ."

"I . . . I . . . I . . . I . . . I . . . ! That's what I mean. Eyeballs turned inward. That your idea of progress?"

"Got any better ideas?"

"Yeah, all that self-discipline or whatever . . . that made you so sick . . . why can't you use the same thing to get well?"

Rosemary stared up at Trudy. She'd never thought about that. Trudy had a point . . . a good one. No, it was wild . . . crazy!

"Well," Trudy said, "answer me that one."

But Rosemary couldn't think of an answer. In a way, Trudy made sense. If she *could* direct all her energies to getting well . . no, it wouldn't work. But still. . . .

"I'm waiting," Trudy said. "Answer me . . . if you can."

Rosemary suppressed a smile. "Could you repeat the question?"

Trudy sighed and started in. "That discipline. That iron will you keep talking about. . . ." She stopped when she saw Rosemary smile.

GOODBYE, PAPER DOLL 151

For a moment the two of them just looked at each other. Then they both grinned, pretending not to notice the other's moist eyes.

Trudy cleared her throat. "Gotta go," she said, but at the door, she stopped and turned. "Oh, I almost forgot to tell you his name."

"Whose name?"

"The fish, stupid."

"What is it?"

"Moby Dick, what else?" She crossed her eyes, pursed her lips, sucked in her cheeks and left Rosemary laughing.

Still chuckling, Rosemary looked over at the fish. It was circling around and around in its bowl, never getting anywhere. Just like a soap opera, going on and on and on. Getting nowhere. Making no progress.

She dialed Jason's telephone number. There was no answer. She hung up.

She looked around the room, at the drawn drapes, the blank TV set, the closed closet. She stared at the IV bottle, at her arm tied down. She raised herself up and carefully slid the IV needle out of her arm, and then rang the call button.

Chris came into the room smiling. "Fairy godmother reporting for duty. Your wish is my command. Just name it and . . ." Then she saw what Rosemary had done. "That's the second time you've aborted your IV. Means surgery, you know."

"I don't need it anymore," Rosemary said evenly.

Chris looked at her suspiciously. "What are you up to? If you're thinking of running away, forget it."

"Bring me a tray."

"What?"

"A tray . . . food. I want to eat."

Gravely, Chris looked into Rosemary's eyes. Then her attitude changed. "Sure?"

"Sure," Rosemary said.

But when the tray came, she sat frozen. She looked down at it, unable to move.

Chris sat on the bed. "Come on, Rosemary," she said, picking up the fork. "I'll help you." She dipped the fork into the mashed potatoes. "A little at a time . . . a tiny bite . . . just a bite."

Rosemary clenched her fists, closed her eyes tightly and let Chris put the fork into her mouth. She swallowed without chewing, feeling the lump of food go down. She wanted to retch as the nausea rose.

"Take a big breath," Chris said, scooping up more food. "Breathe deeply." Then she fed Rosemary another mouthful.

This time the food went down a little easier. Rosemary opened her eyes and tried for a smile, but her body was bathed in perspiration. She gulped down another mouthful.

"Good girl," Chris prodded gently. "That's the way."

Another forkful and Chris grinned. "You're on your way . . . terrific . . . great . . . that's my baby."

While Chris dipped the next forkful into the gravy Rosemary shuddered. And as Chris continued to feed her, she forced herself to think of something else. Over and over in her own mind she murmured: . . . take a baby step . . . a baby step . . . a giant step.

And then there was the eating by herself. The days of chewing, the terror. The swallowing, the stark fear. The rich milkshakes, the bloated feeling. The urge to throw up, but holding it down.

And finally, with Chris's encouragement, with Dr. Collen's direction, with Dr. Feinstein's congratulations, and with her family's applause, Rosemary began to gain weight.

It was still painful for her to walk. But she wasn't thinking of herself as she hobbled up the tree-lined drive to Jason's house. She had achieved the necessary weight gain to leave the hospital in record time. And now, as she walked toward the house, all she could think of was Jason. His pain, his grief, his cruel loss.

Before she reached the door, the Countess flung it open. Rosemary stopped. Her mind raced backward. This was not the lady she remembered. The Countess's hair was disheveled, stray wisps straggling down her neck. Her hand shook as she reached out to Rosemary, and her face was streaked with tears. This was the fragile old lady Rosemary had envisioned before she had met her.

"Thank you," she said, as Rosemary embraced her. "Thank you for coming. Perhaps you can do something with him. I can't... I can't."

Rosemary held her arm around the Countess's waist as they entered the house.

"Jason's not a quitter. It'll be all right," said Rosemary gently.

"Oh, I hope so. He still won't come out of his room. He hasn't eaten a thing for days." She dabbed at her eyes with a handkerchief. "I don't know what to do. Oh, dear God, I don't know what to do...."

Rosemary kissed her. "I'll go in to see him."

"Do you want me to tell him you're here first?"

"He might say no. I'll just go in, okay?"

The Countess nodded.

Rosemary was frightened. If Jason threw her out, he'd have good reason. As she walked to his room, she thought of the dozens of times she had tried to reach him by phone. But now, even if he wouldn't talk to her, he'd have to listen.

But what would she say? What could she tell him that would help? The pounding of her heart rang in her ears as she opened his door.

The room was dark and musty smelling. As her eyes adjusted to the darkness, she made out Jason's form on the bed. His back toward her, he was facing the wall.

Rosemary walked to the bed and sat on it. She put her hand on his hair. "It's me," she said quietly.

His body tightened, but he didn't answer. There was an untouched tray of food on his bedside table.

Rosemary looked around the room. It obviously hadn't been straightened up in days. "Jason, let me talk to you. Please."

He moved closer to the wall. Out of her reach.

Rosemary stood up. He didn't want her there. He hated her. She couldn't blame him.

She started for the door then her eyes scanned something peculiar under the windows. She moved closer. Side-by-side, meticulously arranged, were dozens of pictures of Jason's father.

She dropped to her knees to study the display. A candlestick stood at each end of the arrangement. Starting at the upper left corner was a photo of his father as a small boy. The rest of the pictures were in chronological order. Stacked beside the arrangement was a pile of wrapped Christmas gifts. Tags on them read: "To Dad with love, Jason."

It was like a shrine! Jason had made a shrine to his father.

Tears springing to her eyes, Rosemary went back and sat on the bed. This time she didn't touch Jason. "I love you," she said. "Oh, Jason, I love you more than anyone."

Jason didn't move.

"I know you don't love me anymore. Why should you?" Rosemary said. "I've been rotten . . . and selfish. If you don't ever want to see me again, that's okay. I just want you to know I'll never love anyone the way I love you."

She saw Jason's shoulders heave, then heard a sob.

"Please, Jason, just forgive me. I love you. I love you. . . ."

Jason turned to face her. Tears were spilling down his face. He looked up at her. "Rosie," he said hollowly, then reached for her hand.

Her own tears falling onto it, Rosemary raised his hand and kissed it. She held it to her wet cheek.

Then, with her other hand, she picked up the spoon from the tray and dipped it into a dish of custard. She held the spoon to Jason's lips.

For a moment, he hesitated. Then he let her put the custard into his mouth.

Rosemary smiled tremulously as she dipped into the dish for more custard. "One for you," she said as she fed him.

She filled the spoon again and this time tasted the custard herself. "... and one for me."

She picked up the dish and held it between them. "One for you ... and one for me. One for you ... and one for me. One for you ..."

About The Author

In addition to writing books and educational material, Anne Snyder is active in the field of television. She is also a teacher of creative writing, and has taught at Valley College, Pierce College and University of California, Northridge. Her novel, FIRST STEP, published by Signet in paperback, was a winner of the 1976 Friends of American Writers Award. Her novel, MY NAME IS DAVY—I'M AN ALCOHOLIC, is also published by Signet. Her essay, *Using Literature and Poetry Effectively*, appeared in an anthology published by the International Reading Association. She and her husband live in Woodland Hills, California.